THE SECRET

Carol Beach York

SCHOLASTIC INC.
New York Toronto London Auckland Sydney

Cover Photograph by Bernard Vidal

ISBN 0-590-41648-0

12 11 10 9 8 7 6 5 4 3   9/8 0 1 2/9

THE SECRET

A Windswept ® Book

WINDSWEPT® TITLES
FROM SCHOLASTIC

Don't Walk Alone by Mary Bringle
Someone Is Out There by Carole Standish
Girl in the Shadows by Miriam Lynch
The House of Three Sisters
  by Virginia Nielsen
Yesterday's Girl by Madeline Sunshine
The Snow's Secret by Carole Standish
The Red Room by Kaye Dobkin
The Silvery Past by Candice Ransom
Dreams and Memories by Lavinia Harris
A Forgotten Girl by Elisabeth Ogilvie
The Ghost of Graydon Place
  by Dorothy Francis
The Silent Witness by Meredith Hill
The Empty Attic by Jean Francis Webb
Murder by Moonlight
  by Dorothy Woolfolk
The Girl Cried Murder
  by Dorothy Woolfolk
House of Fear by Willo Davis Roberts
Mirror, Mirror by Virginia Nielsen
The Missing Sunrise
  by Joan Oppenheimer
Dark Magic by Miriam Lynch
Mysterious Summer by Marion Schultz
Phantom Light by Susan Dix
The Lost Holiday by Elizabeth Olsen
A Date with Danger
  by Edward Hunsberger
The Burned Letter by Conrad Nowels
The Secret by Carol Beach York

CHAPTER ONE

I suppose I will always have mixed feelings about Aunt Lorna's house. Things that happened there haunt me still in memory.

And yet it was a lovely old house, with a rose garden and a small apple orchard. It was on the edge of town, and the woods bordered lawns so large Mom said it was like living in a park.

Aunt Lorna had hired a gardener to care for the lawns and the flowers and the orchard. He was also a handyman. Mom said it was a perfect arrangement. Aunt Lorna was a widow, and she and Carrie certainly couldn't cope with such a big house and grounds themselves.

Yes . . . a perfect arrangement.

We spent Christmas week at Aunt Lorna's, Mom and Dad and I. It was Aunt Lorna's first Christmas in the house, and our first time to see it. Thinking back, the Christmas visit blurs. Moments come toward me and then recede, wavery and distorted like images in a dream. All the color and gaiety of the holidays. And all the sorrow of the bad part, the secret.

"We'll never tell anyone," my cousin Carrie said, as we stood by the car that cold December day and watched Bonnie Vayle go into a local coffee shop called the Minuette.

"Our secret," I agreed.

Wind swept down Rowen Avenue. Soon it would snow.

When we were leaving Aunt Lorna's after Christmas week, Mom and Dad and I, I heard Mom talking about summer vacation. She and Aunt Lorna were hugging, kissing good-bye, two loving sisters. And they were making plans for another visit when summer came.

Summer's a long way off, I thought, standing dull and miserable by the foot of Aunt Lorna's beautiful sweeping staircase. In the hall around me were our suitcases, ready to be carried out to the car. We were going home — and here was Aunt Lorna saying we had to come back again as soon as school was out. *That's a long way off,* I thought. *I won't worry about it now.*

But it's dumb to try to put things out of your mind because they seem far off. Time passes. Time *flies*. Days go by like you wouldn't believe. The summer vacation that was so far off arrived in a rush. One day it was January; the next day it was June.

It was June sixth.

School closed.

I brought home my gym suit and my books and the padlock for my locker.

I had finished my junior year.

Next year I would be a senior — and I was hopeful that exciting things would result from that fact, like a boyfriend, for instance. I'd never had a special boyfriend. Also when I was a senior, girls in lower classes would look up to me with awe, the way I had looked up to Nancy Patterson and Debbie Keene and Susie O'Brien.

But between junior year and senior year was summer vacation.

I didn't want to visit Aunt Lorna. I never wanted to go to that house or that town again. The only thing was Carrie. I would certainly miss Carrie if I never went back. We always had great times together whenever she visited Elmwood. When we were ten we were experts at baking peanut butter cookies; when we were thirteen we fell in love with the same boy — George Sanderhoff. We walked by his house arm in arm, giggling

3

and casting romantic glances across the uneven patches of grass that made up the Sanderhoffs' front yard.

Yes, I would miss my cousin Carrie, but I made imaginary plans of ways and places I could see her. She could come to Elmwood to visit me; when we graduated we could go to the same college and be roommates; we would support each other in our careers; and someday, when we were both married, we could live in the same town.

I thought of lots of ways I could see Carrie without having to go back to Rowenville. But I knew the vacation plans were made, and I'd have to go.

I guess Carrie was having a lot of the same thoughts I was having. She wrote me a letter just a few days before Mom and I were to leave to visit her and Aunt Lorna. It was hot for June, the day her letter came, and the mail was late. It was nearly two o'clock when the mailman's step sounded sluggish and heavy on the porch.

Mom got the mail and came back through the living room sorting the envelopes and mumbling to herself. "Bills — bills. Oh, here's a letter for you, Elizabeth. From Carrie."

I was watering the plants on the living room windowsill. I could see the peaceful streets of Elmwood from the window. Boys riding on bikes. Mrs. Norris weeding flowerbeds in her yard next door. The Elmwood

4

Public Library was across the street from our house, with a flagpole in the library yard. The flag hung limply in the still summer air. Children sat on the library steps in the sun. Story Hour would begin at two-thirty.

I wanted to stay in Elmwood. I wanted to stay right where I was all summer.

I put the letter from Carrie in the back pocket of my jeans, and went on watering the plants. Mom was opening other mail, and I was glad she didn't ask what Carrie had to say. Carrie didn't write often, but every time she did I was afraid she would say something about what had happened at Christmastime. She never did, but I always worried that she might.

I finished the plants and then, alone in my room, I opened the letter. As soon as I read the first few words, I knew Carrie remembered everything just as vividly as I did. Remembered, and wished we could go back and do it over and make it different.

But you can't ever do that. What's done is done, as Dad likes to say. The letter began:

Dear Elizabeth,
I know you're probably not too eager to come back here, but things will be better this time. They've got to be. Right?

I could picture Carrie's face — pale, intense, bent over the pages of the letter as

5

she wrote. Her room was large, with a sloping ceiling at one end, and a wide window seat where you could sit and look out at the woods behind the house. . . . My room had been like that, too. I had loved the window seat, loved to sit and watch the dark woods and the falling snow. I had felt special, romantic, dreamy at Aunt Lorna's house, sitting by my window watching the snow like the heroine of a Christmas-holiday movie.

At first I felt that way.

But when I looked from the window one last time before we left, I had only felt guilty and horrified, overwhelmed by the burden of the secret I shared with Carrie.

Carrie understood. I knew she did. I could see her sitting in her room, writing to me. There was a photo of Tom on her desk. Beyond her windows the grass would be green, the trees in the apple orchard would have delicate white blossoms. The flower beds would need tending. Aunt Lorna's gardener would be working in this pleasant summery scene — in a place that I wanted to stay as far away from as I possibly could.

The pages of Carrie's letter crinkled between my fingers. It was the only sound in the room.

Oh, Carrie, they've got to be be better, I thought. *They've got to be better.*

The next part of the letter startled me.

* * *

But I wanted to tell you — I think there's something wrong with this house. It's haunted or something. Strange things happen. Honest, Elizabeth. Mother says it's all my imagination, but — well, wait till you come. I'll tell you all the details.

I read the letter over three times. Aunt Lorna's house was haunted? My mind started working. If the house was haunted, maybe Mom wouldn't be so eager to go for a second visit. We could stay at home in Elmwood for the summer. That would be great.

I fiddled with this idea for the rest of the afternoon. When I finally went downstairs it was nearly five o'clock, and Mom asked me to make the salads for dinner.

Dad had already left for the business trip that was going to keep him away for several weeks, the time Mom and I were going to spend at Aunt Lorna's. Mom was alone in the kitchen, except for Sweetie Pie, our canary. Her cage was by the kitchen windows, and she hopped from perch to perch, cocking her head pertly, watching the world with bright, tiny eyes.

Late afternoon sunlight slanted through the windows across the yellow tile of the kitchen floor. I chopped celery and carrots and radishes, thinking how I could best begin telling Mom.

7

"Mom — you know that letter Carrie wrote me? Well, she thinks their house is haunted."

I waited for her reaction.

"Haunted?" Mom looked at me with surprise.

"Yes. She thinks there's something wrong with the house, evil spirits or something."

Carrie hadn't actually said "evil spirits," but when a house was haunted it could be evil spirits, couldn't it? I thought it sounded good.

"Evil spirits?" Mom echoed my words.

I let cold water from the faucet run over the chopped vegetables.

Then I said, "Maybe we shouldn't go to visit. I mean, if there are evil spirits there."

Mom laughed. The moment of surprise was passed. She had absorbed my information and rejected it. "Don't be silly, Elizabeth. There are no evil spirits or haunted houses. You know that."

I felt defeated. I didn't even answer.

"Elizabeth?" Mom looked at me in that way she has. Waiting for me to agree with her.

Finally I said, "Sure, I guess you're right." *Why is life so difficult?* I wondered. *Why don't people understand what you are trying to tell them?*

The kitchen was silent for a few minutes, except for the sounds of dinner preparations.

Mom unwrapped cellophane from a package of dinner rolls. She was frying pork chops, and the pan grated against the burner. I finished the salads. Usually I liked making the salads, thinking of special things to add, like olives or bacon bits or crumbled cheese. But this afternoon all I could think about was Aunt Lorna's house, with the woods around it. And past Aunt Lorna's house, on down a country road, was the skating pond and the old warming house.

"Think how disappointed Aunt Lorna and Carrie would be if we didn't come," Mom said.

She was bustling around the kitchen, busy and cheerful, and I thought, *Oh, Mom, you just don't understand!*

But of course there was no way she could understand. She didn't know what had happened.

"We'll never tell anyone." Carrie's dark hair blew around her face.

Bonnie went into the Minuette.

Far away from where we were, it was cold by the skating house. Snow was beginning to fall.

We'll never tell anyone . . . we'll never tell anyone . . . we'll never tell anyone. . . .

Remembered words echoed in my head.

There was no way Mom could understand, because she didn't know what really happened. Nobody knew.

Dear Diary

I wrote these first words and stopped, tapping my pen, staring at the blank page of the book lying on my desk.

My bedroom window was open and a warm night breeze drifted in. I wondered what Carrie was doing, far away in Rowenville, in a house where strange things were happening.

Dear Diary.— I got a letter from Carrie today. She thinks their house may be haunted.

I stopped again. Carrie hadn't said anything about Tom. Were they still dating? I hoped so, she liked him so much. I tapped the pen against my teeth, thinking about Tom Abbott. He was the cause of so many problems. Were boys always such bad trouble?

I propped my chin on my hand and looked across the room with an absent stare, not really seeing anything. My friend Ginny had a steady boyfriend. So did another friend, Laurene. Carrie had Tom Abbott. Maybe next year when I was a senior I would have a steady boyfriend too.

I got up restlessly, tossing my pen down on the open pages of the diary. I didn't know what I wanted to write. Finally I just turned on the radio and listened to some music while I brushed my hair.

When I was ready for bed I finished the diary entry, but I didn't write much. Sometimes I write *pages*. Not tonight.

Dear Diary — I got a letter from Carrie today. She thinks their house may be haunted. Nothing helps. Mom doesn't understand. I've got to go to Aunt Lorna's.

CHAPTER TWO

The drive to Aunt Lorna's house was a full day's trip. Mom and I started off about eight o'clock. It was a bright, sunny morning. Mrs. Norris waved good-bye from her yard. She was taking care of Sweetie Pie for us while we were gone, and she would take in our mail. Her son would cut our grass. Going away took so many arrangements.

The sunshiny streets of Elmwood dwindled into the distance. Soon we were on the expressway.

We sped along with the usual travelers' accompaniment of radio music and crinkling road maps. I was in charge of the maps for Mom since she hadn't been the driver the first time we went to Aunt Lorna's.

About noon we stopped for lunch, and came out of the restaurant wearing sunglasses, ready for the afternoon drive. But within the hour the sunlight faded. The sky grew overcast and in the air there was the pungent, summertime smell of a coming rain. We went on along the highway to the rhythm of the radio music, while the sky darkened above and I grew more and more lonesome for home.

At four-thirty we arrived in Rowenville, although at first nothing looked familiar. But we saw the sign: WELCOME TO ROWENVILLE. So we knew we were in the right place.

"Here we are," Mom said happily. "We didn't get lost!"

She sounded relieved, and I craned my neck as we drove through the streets, looking this way and that for a glimpse of something I recognized. It all looked so different without the snow. Then we came to Rowen Avenue, which was the main street, and everything was suddenly very familiar. There was the movie theater, Rexall Drugs, other stores I remembered. And the Minuette. The same neon sign was in the window: BEST FOOD IN TOWN.

Mom didn't give the Minuette a glance. It meant nothing to her. We drove past it, and came to a stop at a traffic light at the intersection.

"Young man," Mom called to a tall, blond boy putting a letter into the corner mail box. "Young man. . . ."

My window was only partly down, and I rolled it lower because the boy was on my side of the car. He was very nice-looking, and he came toward us with an agreeable, helpful expression.

"You lost?" he asked, bending to smile in through the open car window.

I felt my cheeks flush. He was so close . . . so suddenly *there* . . . his voice as nice as I could ever hope a boy's voice would be.

"Not lost exactly." Mom leaned forward to talk past me to the boy, who was now resting his arm on the open window. "We want to go to Green Oak Lane — 448 Green Oak Lane."

The boy smiled. He eased himself up and gestured straight ahead. "You make a left turn two blocks up and you'll be on Green Oak. Four-forty-eight should be another mile or so."

"Thanks very much." Mom settled back behind the wheel, and I smiled up self-consciously at the boy.

He was looking at me in a friendly way, and I had the unexpected impression that he was about to say something to me. But our car was already moving away from the curb, and if he was going to say something now it was too late.

I looked back, and he was standing just where we'd left him, hands in his pockets, watching us drive away.

"Wasn't that a nice young man?" Mom was saying. Her eyes were straight ahead, concerned with the turn she would make in two blocks. "Now that he's given us such good directions, I think I remember the way."

We made the left turn and started along Green Oak Lane. I began to fold up the road map I had been holding in my lap. Within a block or so the houses began to thin out. One block had only one house, completely surrounded by trees. Aunt Lorna's house was at the very edge of the town, at the edge of the woods. Beyond her house, Green Oak Lane became Green Oak Road, a two-lane blacktop road going off into the distance through the woods and on to outlying farmhouses.

My thoughts about the nice-looking blond boy faded away as we drew nearer to Aunt Lorna's house. The air had grown close and sultry. Green Oak Lane was dark under the cloudy sky and the great shadows of trees. Too soon this last distance was covered, and Aunt Lorna's house appeared ahead.

"There it is," Mom said, as though I couldn't see the house only too well myself.

I wondered how I had ever thought it was beautiful. But I *had* thought so. When Aunt Lorna left her New York City apartment and bought the house in this far-off little village late last summer, she had taken snapshots and sent them to us. "I've finally found my dream house," she had written in the letter that accompanied the pictures. In the pictures Aunt Lorna had posed Carrie by the front steps of the house, smiling and looking happy.

Brilliant bursts of color from flowers growing in the surrounding yard shimmered in a radiant sunlight.

There were also photos showing the grove of apple trees and a side view of the house. The woods beyond looked cool and green. "You can almost hear the bird calls from the woods," Dad had said, and I couldn't wait to visit this beautiful old house and the flower gardens and apple orchard and woods.

We had pored over the pictures, and Mom had said Carrie was growing up to be a very pretty girl. "Slimming down too," she'd added. You could sort of tell, even in snapshots, that Carrie was quiet and shy, but she did look pretty and very happy smiling in the sunlight. And she looked thinner, although of course she had never been *fat,* just a little plump. (At ten she loved the peanut butter cookies we made; at fifteen she was reading all the diet articles in *Teen Girl* magazine.)

When we had come to visit at Christmastime, the snowy woods and countryside looked even more beautiful to me than in the snapshots Aunt Lorna had sent. There had been heavy snowfalls before we arrived, and the woods behind the house were a fairyland, tree branches lined with white, bushes soft with snow. Bright red berries grew by a rustic bridge over a little stream at the end of the back property where the woods began. The sky rose above, boundless, as winter-white as the world below.

"It's too isolated for me," Mom confided to Dad as we drove up Green Oak Lane that Christmas and for the first time saw Aunt Lorna's house there by the woods at the end of town.

But I loved it. Inside the house there were fireplaces in the living room and dining room, with real log fires burning. There was a wide, carpeted stairway in the front entrance hall, and a narrow stairway at the back of the house that Aunt Lorna said was the servants' stairway when the house was built. Aunt Lorna, of course, didn't really have servants. Just Joseph, the gardener-handyman, and a woman named Pearl who came to clean on Fridays.

The kitchen was huge, with a butler's pantry and a door to the cellar. The bedrooms had those wide window seats where I sat, watching moonlight shine on the woods and on the silent snow-covered lawns around the house.

In the living room there was a tall Christmas tree, already splendidly decorated and glittering with a multitude of tiny colored lights. Carrie and Aunt Lorna had worked a long time on the tree, and their faces glowed with pride as Mom and Dad and I praised the house and the tree and the fireplaces and everything we set eyes on.

We met Joseph, who had cleared the driveway and flagstone walks with a snow-blower before we came, and who helped Dad carry in our suitcases. Joseph didn't have as much to do in the winter months, so we only saw him a time or two while we visited. He was a middle-aged man, graying and solemn-looking. Aunt Lorna's friend Marian Weatherby had found him for Aunt Lorna. She had also found Pearl to clean on Fridays. Pearl was short and plump, and was fond of dusting picture frames and winding the clocks.

Mom got into a fit of giggles when Aunt Lorna told about Pearl's idiosyncrasies. When Mom and Aunt Lorna got together they were like two schoolgirls.

Aunt Lorna's face got very serious, but her eyes were twinkling. "Pearl is wonderful, for all her eccentricities."

Marian Weatherby had been to college with Aunt Lorna. She lived in Rowenville now, and it was while Aunt Lorna and Carrie were visiting her for a few days that Aunt Lorna had found the house on Green Oak Lane. Actually, Marian Weatherby had found it; Aunt Lorna loved to tell the story.

We sat around the living room fire that night, while the grown-ups had cocktails before dinner, and Aunt Lorna told us how it happened. Beyond the windows the frosty winter landscape glimmered in the twilight.

"Marian knew I'd always wanted to live

18

in a quiet little old-fashioned town, and when Carrie and I arrived Marian said she wanted us to see something.

"We all went outside and got into Marian's car, and came driving over here.

"The house was for sale — and once I saw it I couldn't resist it. The apple trees were blossoming, and with the woods all around and these wonderful old fireplaces and lovely big rooms, it seemed like heaven to me. So here we are."

She looked around with delight, and I knew how she felt. I had just arrived, and already I was falling in love with the house and woods and sitting in front of a warm, blazing fireplace.

Carrie was sitting on the floor by the Christmas tree, listening to her mother's story and watching the flickering light of the fire. When Dad asked, "How about you, Carrie? Do you miss the big city?" she looked up and smiled her sweet, shy smile. "Oh, no," she said, "I love it here just as much as Mom does."

I didn't know it then (Carrie didn't get a chance to tell me until we were getting ready for bed that night), but she was also in love with a boy. She loved the new house, and her new high school, and she loved Tom Abbott who sat next to her in English class. Being in love had put a certain shine on her face, a certain light in her eyes. Mom was right, Carrie was growing up to be very pretty.

It had been a wonderful Christmas . . . and then suddenly everything changed. All because of a girl named Bonnie Vayle, and Carrie's boyfriend Tom Abbott . . . the first boyfriend Carrie had ever had.

Now I looked at the house with dread. It looked ugly to me, dark and gloomy in the oppressive sultriness of the approaching summer storm. A few miles farther along, on the road that wound out of town through the woods, was the old skating pond and the tumbledown warming house no one ever used anymore, and I hated thinking about that place.

Grim memories washed over me and I was helpless to stop them. It was summer now, but it had been snowy winter then.

Maybe things would have been different if there hadn't been so much snow.

Or if Carrie and I hadn't done such a dumb thing.

But there was no way to change things now. Bonnie Vayle wasn't ever going to flirt with Tom Abbott again. Or with any boy.

Bonnie Vayle was dead.

CHAPTER THREE

But that was past. Now it was summer. Carrie came running down the porch steps as soon as our car turned into the driveway. Her dark hair tumbled loose around her shoulders, and she lifted her arm to wave to us as she ran.

Aunt Lorna was on the porch too, smiling happily. She loved having visitors, especially Mom.

We got out of the car and everybody hugged everybody. Mom and Aunt Lorna began talking a mile a minute like they hadn't seen each other in a hundred years, and we all trooped up the steps and into the house. Distant thunder rumbled beyond the woods, and Aunt Lorna put her arm around my shoulder. "You're just in time, you two. It's going to storm."

I could smell the special perfume she always wore, a delicate floral scent that was like her signature.

We stood together in the entryway, at the foot of the great stairway. The dark afternoon made everything look eerie, and Aunt Lorna stepped over to the table opposite the stairway and switched on a lamp. Then the hallway looked more cheerful. Light gleamed on the mahogany banister and Mom looked around with approval.

"It's such a lovely house, Lorna," she said. Then she moved toward the living room doorway, and Carrie darted ahead of her, turning on lamps in the living room. Thunder rumbled again.

"We've been on the porch," Carrie said, looking back at us over her shoulder. "We didn't realize how dark it was getting inside the house."

As we went into the living room Mom murmured softly, "Everything's just as beautiful as I remember it."

But the Christmas tree was gone, and there were no logs in the fireplace; instead the hearth was lined with plants and flowers. The room was the same, yet different. Through screened windows I could see green lawns and trees thick with rustling leaves, where before there had been snowy lawns and bare branches dark against winter skies.

Aunt Lorna perched on the arm of the sofa

by the fireplace. "Everything's about the same since you were here before."

She paused a moment and added, "Well, not *every*thing's the same. You know Joseph died."

Mom nodded. "I remember. You wrote me about that."

Carrie stood across the room, so close to a table lamp she looked like an actress in a stage spotlight. She looked at me and then turned toward the windows, lowering her eyes.

"Yes, it was very sad." Aunt Lorna shook her head regretfully. "Well, now we have Max to take Joseph's place. And of course Pearl still comes to clean on Fridays."

Carrie and I went out to the car to bring in the suitcases, and right away I said, "What about this haunted house stuff?" We were alone by the car, but she shook her head and I knew it wasn't the right place or the right time to talk about her letter.

We lifted suitcases from the trunk and I followed Carrie into the house.

"How's Tom?"

"He's fine." Carrie set down a suitcase and smoothed back her dark hair. "He's away with his father for a fishing trip, but he'll be back next week. He said to tell you hello."

We went back out to the car and drove it further along the driveway to the garage at the rear of the house. Carrie and I hadn't seen each other since Christmas, and I knew we were both thinking about Christmas and about Bonnie Vayle, but neither of us wanted to be the first to bring it up. Maybe we'd never talk about it again, I thought, with a flashing vision of years going by and Carrie and I never once even saying the name "Bonnie Vayle."

The garage doors were open, and I pulled in next to Aunt Lorna's green Buick. Carrie was silent as I turned off the ignition and drew out the key.

"Tell me what you meant in your letter about the house being haunted." I lowered my voice, even though we were quite alone.

Light coming through the open door cast a dim aura over the interior of the garage. Aunt Lorna's car loomed in the shadows. It was a good place for a private talk. There was a sense of secrecy about the stillness of everything there in contrast to the brewing storm outside. The sound of thunder echoed over the woods, not so far away this time.

When Carrie started to speak the words came in a rush, like she'd just been waiting to tell somebody — somebody who wouldn't say it was only her imagination, as her mother had said.

"I have this feeling of being followed, watched, like someone or something is *there*, just a few steps behind me, even though I

24

can't see what it is. When I look around, nothing's there — but oh, Elizabeth, *I do feel it*. And it's a creepy feeling."

I stared at Carrie and she stared back with troubled eyes.

"And this is just since Christmas?"

"Not exactly." Carrie shook her head. "It's more like just the last couple of months, just since Joseph died."

"Since Joseph died? You think it's Joseph coming back to haunt the house?"

"It could be. It was only a few weeks after he died that I began to feel something was wrong. I never felt that way about the house before."

Carrie's voice drifted into the murky gloom of the garage, and I sat gripping the car keys on their brass ring.

A haunted house was one thing, scary but vague. But thinking you knew *who* was haunting it was something else entirely. And in the lonely, half-dark garage it seemed easy to believe in ghosts, invisible spirits, footsteps softly behind you when no one was there.

"Joseph died in the woods right behind the house, didn't he?" I remembered the letter Aunt Lorna wrote to us. Would that be why he came back to haunt the house?

"He was walking in the woods out behind the house." Carrie's voice was low. "And he fell down into a ravine."

It gave me a strange feeling as though I myself had lost my footing and plunged down a steep slope of rough, hard ground.

The garage was silent.

"And that killed him?"

Carrie nodded. "It was a pretty deep ravine, and there were some large rocks at the bottom. He had head injuries."

We were silent again. The humid air was oppressive in the garage, and there was a strong smell of oil and gasoline. Suddenly I wanted to get out of the car, out of the garage. It was too close, too warm, too depressing.

"There's more." Carrie touched my arm as I reached for the door handle, but I pushed the handle down. "Let's talk outside, Carrie. It's too hot in here."

We got out of the car, closing the doors with a solid, reassuring slam. As we went outside I noticed the afternoon had grown even darker. There was a threatening stillness in the air that was more menacing than a stormy wind would have been. Leaves hung motionless in the sultry, windless air. Between occasional rumbles of thunder, a silence as complete and eerie as the gathering darkness hung over the countryside.

"What else?" I asked, as we huddled by the garage door. "In your letter you said strange things had happened."

"They *are* strange." There was an insistent

tone in her voice. "Even if my mother says it's my imagination, I know it's *not* my imagination."

I thought how Aunt Lorna would hate to hear anything bad about her wonderful, wonderful house.

"One day I came home from school and Mom had gone to the dentist. She left a note on the hall table, and I was reading it when all of a sudden I had this feeling I should turn around. I don't know why exactly, I must have heard something without even realizing I heard it, or maybe there wasn't even any sound, maybe I just had ESP or something —"

"What, *what?*" I interrupted impatiently. *I* was in that deserted entryway with Carrie, reading Aunt Lorna's note: "Carrie, I have gone to the dentist. Be home soon."

What made Carrie turn? What happened when she turned?

Her next words surprised me.

"It was a chair, Elizabeth. When I turned around and looked up, a chair was flying down the stairs toward me — straight at me."

A chair. I was taken aback for a moment. I had thought maybe Carrie was going to turn and see a real ghost behind her, something really weird, anything, not just something as ordinary as a chair.

"A chair?" My voice was cautious.

"Oh, Elizabeth, please believe me." Carrie

was distressed. "It was a chair that we have in the upstairs hall, and Mom said it probably got set too close to the top of the stairs and fell down. She said the one thing Pearl isn't too particular about is getting things back in just the right place when she vacuums, and the chair was just too close to the stairs."

This time we didn't stop to laugh about Pearl.

But still, at first, a chair didn't seem all that scary to me. And who knows, I thought, maybe Aunt Lorna's theory was right and the chair had just been put too close to the top of the stairs.

Carrie knew what I was thinking, and she began shaking her head. "When something falls down the stairs it falls *down the stairs*. Right?"

I wasn't sure what she meant, but she hurried on.

"This chair wasn't falling on the stairs, it wasn't touching the stairs. It was sailing through the air — straight at me."

A chair that was sailing through the air — straight at somebody — began to seem rather scary after all. It began to seem like something I didn't like very much.

"I jumped out of the way," Carrie said. "But only just in time. The chair crashed against the wall by the living room doorway and then everything was very still, but I had the feeling someone — something — was watching me. I couldn't stay in the house. I went out and waited in the yard until my mother came home. Then," Carrie made a face, "we had the big discussion about how the chair might have been too close to the top of the stairs."

"But you said it was flying through the air, not even touching the stairs."

"It was," Carrie said. "But my mother said, 'Don't be silly, Carrie, that couldn't happen.'"

I didn't feel like saying, "Don't be silly, Carrie." Part of me wanted to go home to Elmwood more than ever. Another part of me wanted to know what else had happened that was strange.

"One night I started to do some homework," Carrie leaned close to me as she spoke, "and when I opened my history book there was this newspaper clipping, the picture of Joseph that had been in the paper when he died. It was a picture taken when he was a few years younger. There he was all of a sudden, smiling at me in my history book. It made me feel like he was right there in the room with me or something. Really weird, Elizabeth.

"Mom said I probably cut out the picture at the time of his accident, and forgot that

I'd stuck it in my book. Now why would I want to do that!" Carrie gestured with exasperation.

"You think Joseph put it there himself — I mean Joseph's ghost?"

"I don't know," Carrie said. "Maybe so. Another time I was in my room, sitting on the window seat reading, when I heard my name called — well, not like my mom was calling me from downstairs or anything like that. It was mysterious, drawn-out. 'Ca-a-r-rie.' Like a sigh floating in the air. My door was half open and as I looked up it swung shut with a terrible bang. I nearly jumped out of my skin."

"Just slammed shut by itself?"

Carrie nodded. "Just slammed shut by itself. I was scared silly and when I told my mother she said it must have been a draft. A draft!" Carrie looked exasperated again. "Honest, Elizabeth, it was a peaceful, calm, spring day. There wasn't a bit of wind anywhere. Where would a draft come from? No, it wasn't a draft at all."

I thought about that, looking across the lawn toward the house shrouded by trees in the shadowless light of the approaching storm. There was still no rain, but lightning flashed and Carrie said, "Come on, we'd better get to the house before the rain starts."

I walked with her along the flagstone path

that led from the gravel driveway to the front steps. She kept her eyes down as though she didn't want to look at the house, and I knew she didn't like the house any better than I did. Something had been spoiled for both of us, and Aunt Lorna's beautiful house wasn't beautiful any longer.

Thunder rumbled again.

"Come on, rain, if you're going to." Carrie looked up defiantly at the sky.

We were almost to the porch steps.

"What happened when the door slammed closed?" I asked. "Were you trapped in your room?"

Carrie was looking down again, watching her own feet on the flagstone walk. "No, there's no lock on my door. It took me a little while to get up enough courage to go over and try to open it. I didn't know what might be out in the hallway."

I nodded, shivering despite the warmth of the afternoon.

"By and by I got more scared of staying alone in the room with that closed door than I was scared of opening the door," Carrie admitted. "So I went over and I listened, and I couldn't hear anything in the hall. So I opened the door. My heart was jumping around, but the hall was empty. There was nothing there."

She looked at me with a half-hearted

smile. "Same old story: When I look, no one's there."

We were almost to the house. I could see lamplight from the lower windows, the living room windows. A mournful cast of early evening light lay over the woods, the lawns, the road out of town. No car went by. No bird sang.

And no rain fell yet.

CHAPTER FOUR

The rain came as we were eating dinner that evening.

The fine china plates were pale ivory rimmed with gold. The water glasses were Waterford crystal. Aunt Lorna had brought these beautiful things from her New York apartment.

We had decided to dress up for dinner, and I was wearing my white skirt and my favorite green silk blouse. I had a long gold chain with a green pendant, and I felt very fashionable and glamorous sitting at Aunt Lorna's dining room table.

Candles lit in silver candlesticks began to flicker, at first only a little, and then with increasing fervor. The flames leaned down sideways as the wind came at last, billowing draperies at the dining room windows, blowing out the candles, flapping the lacy tablecloth.

"What a storm!" Aunt Lorna exclaimed.

Carrie's dark hair and eyes looked darker than ever above the white ruffle of her blouse.

There was a general flurry to leave the table and close windows.

Slanting lines of rain swept across the lawns. Lightning crackled in the sky, flooding the countryside with split seconds of blinding light.

I had never seen such a storm in all my life. When the windows were closed I returned to the table and sat uneasily, watching the deluge of water sweeping across the panes of glass.

Some vengeful god was out there pouring an ocean of water against the windows.

We could hardly see out.

Carrie brought matches from the kitchen and Aunt Lorna relit the candles. She lifted the lighted match solemnly to the candles like a ceremony.

"Isn't this something," Mom declared, as the candles flickered back to life.

"I ordered a wild storm for your arrival." Aunt Lorna made a flamboyant gesture. She looked out toward the side lawn just as another flash of lightning came down from the sky.

It was just the sort of night *not* to be in a haunted house.

Carrie lifted her eyes and looked across the table at Mom.

"Aunt Frances, did you know this house is haunted?"

"Carrie!" Aunt Lorna's gentle face was distressed. "What a thing to say!"

Mom glanced at Aunt Lorna, and then at me.

"Did you know that, Aunt Frances?" Carrie persisted.

Mom smiled at Carrie. "Elizabeth said —"

But Aunt Lorna interrupted.

"Carrie, I wish you would stop talking like that."

She sounded unhappy. She had found the house of her dreams, and Carrie wanted to bring in a ghost.

Joseph's ghost?

I tried to remember Joseph better, but he was only a middle-aged, gray-haired man in my memory. He smiled at me. He was nice. Was I forgetting something? Was there more to remember about Joseph?

Mom laughed to ease the tension. "That's all right, Lorna. A marvelous old house like this ought to have a few superstitions attached to it. Gives it atmosphere."

Aunt Lorna's sense of humor returned. She smiled as she said, "On stormy nights like this, the house has quite enough atmosphere on its own."

I was willing to agree with Aunt Lorna. With the thunder and lightning and wind and rain, the house was already besieged enough by threatening forces, without adding the supernatural.

Mom and Aunt Lorna began to talk about other things, and I stared at my own reflection in the dark, gleaming dining room windows.

Did I believe in haunted houses?

Did I believe that Carrie was followed in her own house, watched by invisible eyes, frightened by a slamming door, attacked by a chair?

I wondered what Ginny and Laurene were doing back in Elmwood. Laurene was probably out with her boyfriend, and Ginny was probably at Dairy Queen.

I wanted so much to be back in my house in Elmwood. I wanted to hear the phone ring and have Mom or Dad call me and tell me it was Ginny, or Laurene, or whoever.

I wanted to be home, and grab the phone and say, "Hi!"

The room I had was the same one I'd had at Christmastime. The carpet was a warm olive-green, and there was an old-fashioned writing table where I sat to write in my diary. Aunt Lorna had bought some furniture from the family who sold her the house, and the writing table was one of the pieces. There was a brass lamp on the table, and a drawer for my diary.

Of course the best part of the room was that window seat.

I was getting ready for bed when Carrie came. She brushed her hair while we talked. It was almost like a pajama party back in Elmwood, except that nothing at Aunt Lorna's house was quite like Elmwood.

The worst of the storm was over. Rain pattered softly at the half-opened windows. Droplets clung and glittered on the dark mesh of the window screen.

The air was cooler. The thunder and lightning were gone.

Carrie fingered a stray lock of hair and looked at me intently. "Elizabeth? Do you feel anything strange about this house since you came? I know you haven't been here very long, but do you feel anything like what I was talking about?"

On a dark, rainy night it was easy to believe in ghosts and evil spirits and haunted houses. You expected creaking floorboards and the sound of loose shutters banging in the wind.

It was easy to imagine all sorts of things on a stormy night. Through the open windows, the woods and the countryside seemed to come indoors with us, bringing all the unknown things that lurked outside.

"It's kind of scary here," I admitted.

Carrie's eyes were enormous in the lamplight. "It *is* scary." She seized my words at once. "And I have to live here. How would you like that?"

I knew I wouldn't like that very much at all.

And then I thought of something I liked even less. I hated to even mention it.

"Carrie . . . did you ever think it might be Bonnie's ghost, not Joseph's?"

She seemed to shrink away from my words, and I said, "Well, it could be, couldn't it?"

"But Bonnie didn't know what we *did*," Carrie said doubtfully. "Why would she want to haunt this house?"

"Maybe somehow she *did* know," I reasoned wildly. "Maybe she suspected us."

It didn't make a lot of sense, and we both felt confused.

"Oh, Elizabeth, if only we'd never —" Carrie's voice faded away with the sentence unfinished. After a moment she said wearily, "Whoever or whatever it is, I wish it would stop. Every time I'm in my room I wonder if the door's going to slam shut again. If I open a book I wonder if I'm going to see Joseph's face staring up at me. Every time I start up the stairs, I wonder if that chair is going to come flying down at me."

It was Carrie's house. I could go home in a few weeks, but Carrie had to stay.

"That chair is still in the hallway?"

Carrie nodded. "It's still there. But it's farther down the hall, away from the stairs. Mom made sure of that. You didn't notice it?"

I shook my head. Carrie watched as I set down my hairbrush and went to the bedroom door. When I opened the door I could see a lamp lit on a table near the head of the stairway. The chair, which had been beside the table, was now several feet away, almost opposite my door. The chair looked misplaced, estranged from its spot beside the table.

There was certainly no way the chair could accidentally fall downstairs now. It would have to go a long way before it was even near the top of the stairs.

Table, lamp, . . . chair. I stood looking at the hallway a moment longer, and then came back into my room.

Carrie was sitting cross-legged at the foot of my bed. Her hair glowed in the lamplight.

"The chair looks okay to me," I said encouragingly. "Anyway, it's a lot better where it is."

Carrie didn't answer at first. Then she said, "I suppose so," but she didn't sound convinced. She slid down from her perch at the foot of the bed. On her way back to her own room, she paused at the doorway and said, "Tom's birthday is next week. Want to go shopping with me tomorrow and buy him a birthday present?"

"Sure," I said. "That sounds fine to me."

"Okay. See you in the morning."

The door opened, closed; Carrie was gone. I was alone . . . and all the things Carrie had told me that afternoon were hard to get off my mind.

Dear Diary (I wrote) — We are at Aunt Lorna's. Carrie thinks Joseph has come back to haunt the house. Someone — or something — watches her, follows her, but when she looks, nothing is there. I wish I were back home.

Without turning out the light I got into bed and lay very still, listening to the sounds of the rainy night outside. The last drops slid down the windowpanes, sparkling in the lamplight.

Finally I turned off the bedside lamp.

Think about something nice before you go to sleep. That's what Mom always said.

Think about something nice before you go to sleep.

The only nice thing I could think of was the blond boy who had given us directions.

"You lost?" he said, leaning toward the car window.

I hoped someday I would see him again.

CHAPTER
FIVE

The storm had torn branches from some of the trees around the house, and in the morning when I looked out of my window I saw a man in a gray cotton shirt and work pants clearing up the debris. I watched a few minutes as he gathered fallen branches and put them into a wheelbarrow. *That must be Max,* I decided, *Aunt Lorna's new gardener.*

The rain had stopped during the night, but the sky was still overcast and it seemed likely there would be rain again before the day was over.

Peony bushes along the driveway had been devastated by the storm. Pink petals covered the damp ground around the bedraggled bushes. I was thinking how vulnerable the fragile flowers were when a jaunty robin hopping across the grass cheered me up. He stopped and pecked at the grass, although I couldn't see if he had found himself a worm or not.

Eventually I turned away from the window and thought about what I would wear to go shopping with Carrie for Tom's birthday present. Maybe we would see that boy again . . . that would be nice.

I stood looking at the clothes I had unpacked and hung in the closet the night before.

It was silly to think I'd see one particular person out of a whole townful of people.

Nevertheless, I decided to wear my jeans and favorite green knit top. Green was flattering to my blue-green eyes and dark blond hair.

I even had a green hairband to hold back my hair.

I put my comb, wallet, and lipstick into a straw shoulder-strap bag and looked at my reflection in the mirror over the bureau.

I was ready.

There was something gloomy about the house, even in the morning light. There were shadows in the upper hallways and on the stairs. Reflections lurked on the polished surface of dark woodwork.

The first thing I saw as I left my room was the chair I had looked at the night before. It had been empty then. Now there was a doll sitting in the chair, smiling at me and holding out her arms. I recognized it as the antique doll Carrie kept on her bed, where it sat with its back to the pillows, long skirts spread out over the bedspread. It was a pretty doll, with a delicate china face and golden curls sticking out at the edges of a fancy bonnet trimmed with ribbons.

Then I saw that there was something in the doll's lap, a colorful shiny square . . . a photograph of Carrie. I picked it up with surprise. It was a copy of the photograph Aunt Lorna had sent us when she first moved into the house: Carrie standing by the porch steps in the sunlight with all the flowers bursting with color around her. It had been a beautiful picture, but now it was torn straight down the middle of Carrie's body, a jagged tear starting at the top of the photo and going almost to the bottom.

It gave me a queer feeling to see Carrie's smiling face torn in two, and I stood holding the mutilated picture and wondering what to do. The blue glass eyes of the doll gazed up at me. The painted china mouth smiled.

I heard Carrie's voice from the foot of the stairs . . . "I'm going up to see if Elizabeth's awake yet."

I didn't want Carrie to see the picture; I knew she wasn't the one who had put it there. I stuffed the photo into the pocket of my jeans, just as Carrie appeared at the top of the stairs. She saw the doll right away and she stopped, stared at it, and then came walking slowly toward me.

"How did that get here?"

I shook my head to show I didn't have any idea.

"It's my doll," she said, and I nodded. Neither one of us hurried to pick up the doll and take it back to sit on Carrie's bed.

"Now why is that here?" Carrie persisted, looking at me with an anxious expression.

She didn't really expect an answer.

"Leave it there then," she said with a toss of her head. She backed away a step.

"Are you going to tell your mom?" I asked.

Carrie didn't answer at once. "What's the use," she said finally. "She'd say I put it there and forgot."

We stood looking at the doll, and I think we were both remembering a better reason for not saying anything about the doll. I think we were both wondering if the ghost of Bonnie Vayle had carried the doll from Carrie's room and put it on the chair, that particular chair. And talking to Aunt Lorna about Bonnie Vayle was something we couldn't ever do.

"Oh, come on, let's go downstairs." Carrie twitched away from the vapid gaze of the doll.

Then impulsively she turned back, snatched up the doll, and ran along the hallway to her own room. I felt inside the pocket of my jeans to be sure the snapshot wasn't making a suspicious bulge; almost at once Carrie was back.

We went down the stairs in silence.

In the dining room the chandelier was lit over the table, set for breakfast with yellow potteryware. We slipped into our places feeling secretive and self-conscious, as though our mothers could know by just looking at us that there was something we weren't telling.

But they didn't notice anything unusual.

We ate breakfast. Juice, cold cereal, toast with strawberry jam; Mom passed her coffee cup to Aunt Lorna for a refill; everything was very normal.

When Carrie said we were going shopping to buy Tom a birthday present, Aunt Lorna said we should take her car. "It's a long walk to Rowen Avenue," she explained to Mom, who was pouring cream into her coffee. "And it looks like rain again."

It *was* a long walk. How well I remember *that*. Too long a walk on a bitter cold December night. I felt irritation at these memories. Why were they always coming back to nag at me?

As Carrie and I went to the garage to get the car, we could see Max with his wheelbarrow at the back of the property, by the stream and the little bridge. He was tossing twigs and branches into the wheelbarrow. I wondered if the ravine where Joseph had fallen was nearby, or further out of town.

But I should have been wondering about Max. I should have been warned by the way he looked up as we went into the garage, and was still watching when we drove out. He stood in the overcast gardens of Aunt Lorna's house and watched as we drove away.

I didn't think anything of it. Sometimes we learn things too late. I was busy trying to forget what had happened when I was at Aunt Lorna's house before. I was trying to get into the "now" of it; and the "now" of it was that Carrie and I were going shopping to buy Tom Abbott a birthday present.

Carrie backed out of the driveway onto Green Oak Lane. It was quiet, deserted under the cloudy sky. I didn't even see anybody in a front yard or on a porch, much less walking on the sidewalks.

Then a girl appeared walking a dog, and Carrie slowed the car and called, "Hi."

"She's from school," Carrie said.

The girl waved back.

We drove on another block or so.

"We'll be seniors in September." I looked over at Carrie. "Are you looking forward to that?"

"Sure I am." Carrie gave me one of her shy smiles. After a moment she added, "Then college. How about you, Elizabeth? What are you going to major in?"

The houses of Green Oak Lane went past, their lawns dark and damp from the storm the night before. There were tree branches scattered here too, scattered on the lawns of the houses on Green Oak Lane.

"I'm not sure what I'll major in," I said. "Maybe history. I like history a lot."

"That sounds good," Carrie said. "What do you want to be when you, quote, grow up, unquote."

What did I want to be when I grew up?

Alive, I thought. It was a hard, sudden word out of the dark summer morning.

Bonnie Vayle was dead. Elizabeth March wanted to be alive.

I want to be alive when I grow up. But I remained silent.

We had reached the end of Green Oak Lane. Carrie turned onto Rowen Avenue, and traffic picked up. There, just ahead, was the Minuette, and a parking space almost right in front.

"We're in luck," Carrie said as she edged the car into the space.

In luck indeed. The boy who had given Mom and me directions to Green Oak Lane was just coming out of the coffee shop.

I didn't know if the boy would recognize me or remember me, but I remembered him. I could have recognized him out of a cast of

48

thousands. Blond hair, blue eyes, terrific smile.

He stood for a moment under the striped awning of the coffee shop, and then he started to walk toward our car.

Carrie had hopped out to put money in the parking meter. She looked over from the meter with surprise when she heard the boy speaking to me.

"Haven't we met before?"

He was lounging against the car, his arm on the open window, just as he had done the day when Mom asked him directions to Green Oak Lane. He was suddenly *there* again. So close I couldn't think of one single thing to say.

I sat there in the jeans and green top I'd chosen. I'd hoped to see him. But I couldn't think of a thing to say.

"Did you find that house on Green Oak Lane?"

Out of the corner of my eye I could see Carrie at the parking meter, watching us with interest.

"Yes, we found it. Your directions were just fine."

"Uh-huh." The boy nodded thoughtfully. I looked down and twiddled with the strap of my purse.

"Actually, you know, we're really old friends," the boy said.

He had a confident tone I liked. When I looked up he was smiling at me, nodding his head.

"Sure. We go back a long way. You just don't remember."

I looked at him blankly. What was he talking about?

"We're old friends," he said again, in that wonderful voice.

I tried to stay cool. "How can we be old friends? I don't even know you."

"Greg Preston." He held out his hand to me. "Now you know me."

"Elizabeth March." His hand grasped mine. It was so incredible that I was talking to and shaking hands with this good-looking boy I thought I'd never see again.

Still, I didn't understand what he meant about our being old friends, and he caught my puzzled look.

"I saw you in there one afternoon." He motioned over his shoulder toward the Minuette. "It was way last winter, but I don't forget pretty girls."

I looked past him toward the coffee shop. Below the awning a pallid light glinted on the windows. I had only been in the Minuette twice in my whole life. Once in the early evening, then again one afternoon. Both times held bad memories.

Greg Preston was smiling as though seeing

me in the Minuette had been a happy occasion for him.

"I was home from college last Christmas for the mid-term break, and I saw you in there. I especially remember the day."

He lounged against the car companionably.

Carrie had spent about as much time as she could lingering at the parking meter, trying to look interested in passing cars. Finally she stepped over toward us. Greg straightened up.

"Hello, there."

Carrie smiled shyly, and I told Greg, "This is my cousin Carrie."

"Any friend of Elizabeth's is a friend of mine," Greg said, grinning.

Carrie looked at me and we both smiled. I could see she liked Greg right off. Anybody would like Greg!

"Carrie lives in that house on Green Oak Lane my mom and I were trying to find yesterday. We're visiting there for a few weeks."

"Ah." Greg nodded as though pieces of a puzzle were falling into place. Then he asked Carrie, "If you live on Green Oak Lane, how come I don't know you from school?"

"Last year was my first year here," Carrie explained, and Greg nodded; last year he had been away for his first year of college.

"Do you know Tom Abbott?" Carrie asked. "He was a senior last year. He'll be going to college this fall."

"Sure I know Tom."

It was all very nice, very pleasant. Greg's easy offhand manner made me forget the gloomy feeling of Aunt Lorna's house. It made me forget for a while the leaden skies above the woods where Joseph died.

As I got out of the car Greg held the door for me. "You don't remember me from that afternoon in the coffee shop?" He shook his head reproachfully, but I knew he was teasing.

I had a lot of memories of the afternoon I was in the coffee shop, but not one of them was a memory of seeing Greg. If he was there, I hadn't seen him. The thing I remembered about that afternoon was talking with Carrie about Bonnie, making our plan, writing the note. I remembered Janette, the waitress, in the background of things, so to speak; I did remember her. Curly black hair, a dimpled smile, pink and white striped apron. She brought our tea. Other customers came and went. Someone came past and sat in the next booth. Was that Greg? I really hadn't noticed anybody special that day. But Greg Preston had been there.

"No," I apologized, "I don't remember seeing you."

"That's okay," Greg said, but as I started to move away with Carrie, he put his hand on my arm.

"How about a movie some night?"

I felt overcome with romance and fate! Carrie shot me a quick, eloquent glance, and then looked away like she didn't know Greg and I existed. I tried to sound nonchalant. "Sure, maybe sometime."

"Maybe sometime?" Greg repeated my words with a touch of disappointment. "Maybe sometime?"

I felt embarrassed. "Maybe sometime soon," I said, hoping that would sound better.

Greg instantly swept off an imaginary cowboy hat. "Thank you, Miss Elizabeth. May I call you at your home?"

I scribbled Aunt Lorna's phone number on the back of an envelope Greg had, thinking to myself, *please do call me!*

I wanted to stay there by the car talking to him. But of course I couldn't do that forever.

Greg couldn't either. "Time for me to get to work," he announced, folding the envelope with my phone number and putting it in his pocket. "I've got a summer job working three days a week at Gilley's Hardware."

I smiled brightly, as though I knew all about Gilley's Hardware, and as Greg went off in one direction, Carrie and I went in the other.

"He's so good-looking!" Carrie whispered, slipping her arm through mine. "Do you want to go out with him?"

"How can you ask!"

Carrie laughed, but her thoughts soon went back to her own romance. "I don't know what to get Tom. Boys are hard to buy presents for." I was listening, but I was also thinking about the afternoon Greg said he saw me in the Minuette. Carrie and I thought we were so smart that day, composing our note.

Meet me at the old skating pond at four o'clock.

Our note. It had been such a great idea.

"What can we lose?" I had asked Carrie, as the gray winter afternoon pressed in at the windows of the coffee shop.

I turned to look back. Greg was almost out of sight. As I watched, he turned a corner a block away and disappeared from view.

He was nice. So nice.

Carrie turned into a men's shop, and I followed her, concerned with my own thoughts. We went past the clothing racks to a section marked His Corner, where gift items were sold. Carrie looked at a lot of things, and eventually decided on a set of soap and aftershave in a scent she liked, in a beautiful wooden box.

"Do you think Tom will like it?" It was an important decision for her, and I tried to bring my thoughts back from that long ago

December afternoon when Greg Preston had first seen me.

"Tom will love it," I said, and Carrie touched the box that enclosed the set gently.

"Okay then," she said. "I'll get it."

"A wise choice," the salesman said with enthusiasm. He led us toward the cash register counter. "Would you like this gift-wrapped?"

"Oh, yes, thank you." Carrie looked a little flushed with the excitement of her purchase. It was the first time she had ever bought a birthday present for a boy.

CHAPTER
SIX

When we came out of the bright shop Rowen Avenue looked rather forlorn in the overcast light. There were puddles in the gutter from the storm the night before. Even the neon sign in the Minuette window, BEST FOOD IN TOWN, looked pale and cheerless. I wondered what Greg Preston was doing now — probably waiting on some lucky customer at Gilley's Hardware. It seemed funny to have a sense of missing him when I hardly even knew him.

We drove home along Green Oak Lane, and as we turned into the driveway Carrie said impulsively, "Elizabeth, let's go and see how steep that ravine is, where Joseph fell."

"You've never seen it?"

Carrie shook her head. "I never went into that part of the woods. There's a path over there —" she pointed to one side of the backyard, "and Mom and I used to walk along

56

that sometimes, but not very far. It dwindles away into nothing, and we just didn't think it was smart to go on deep into the woods by ourselves. But Joseph liked to walk in the woods. He was sort of a bird-watcher, he told me once. The ravine's over in that section." She pointed to the opposite end of the yard. "I've never been there at all."

"Not even after his accident?"

"Especially after his accident." Carrie shivered.

The yard was deserted now. Max had finished picking up the fallen branches and he was nowhere in sight. We could see lights in the house, because of the darkness of the day, but Mom and Aunt Lorna didn't come out to welcome us back from shopping. They were probably talking in the living room, not even aware that we had returned.

We got out of the car and walked across the backyard. There was a narrow flagstone path that led to the little stream and the wooden bridge. We went across the bridge, which was like a child's bridge, only a few feet wide and about ten feet across. The stream was shallow, and the bridge was obviously just for effect. Another time I would have thought it was charming. But not today.

Beyond the bridge the woods were lushly green and damp from the rain. The traces of a path were plastered with wet fallen leaves, which saved us from getting into a lot of muddy ground.

"How far do we have to go?" I asked doubtfully. I wasn't sure I really wanted to go into these unfamiliar, rain-drenched woods.

"Not far," Carrie said. "At least that's what Mom said. She went there with the police once, after they found Joseph."

We picked our way along the trail of soggy leaves, and the woods darkened around us. I thought maybe we wouldn't find the ravine, but we did, its steeply sloping sides spotted with small bushes and trees with exposed roots. At the bottom there were large rocks and what had once perhaps been a streambed but was now a weedy, sandy path along the floor of the ravine.

We stood staring down, and it looked easy enough to me for someone to lose their footing and slip if they went too close to the edge. Carrie and I stayed well back. I held my arm around a tree trunk just to be extra safe.

Wild violets grew in the ravine and there were areas of light coming through gaps in the over-hanging trees. I felt nervous looking down the scrubby side of the decline, and I thought how kind of spooky it was that Joseph had only come for a pleasant walk to see birds — and had died.

We went back through the woods, subdued

by the ravine. We crossed the wooden bridge and went single file along the narrow flagstone path through the yard. Max had reappeared and was raking in the side yard. In addition to the fallen branches, there were leaves and small twigs still to be cleaned up.

I was surprised to notice, now that I was closer to Max, that he was quite young. I suppose I had expected another middle-aged man like Joseph, but the new gardener looked only a few years older than Greg Preston.

"Hi." Carrie waved across the yard, but she didn't rush me over to meet him, which I thought was a little odd. I was going to be around for several weeks, and it seemed logical that we'd walk over and she'd say, "This is my cousin Elizabeth," and then we'd talk about the storm the night before and how the yard needed cleaning up, something like that.

Max waved back to acknowledge Carrie's greeting, but he didn't say anything. He stood watching us as Carrie stopped at the car in the driveway and brought the present for Tom with her up the porch steps.

I could feel him watching us both.

"How do you like your new gardener?" I said under my breath, although Max was too far across the yard to overhear.

"Not a whole lot," Carrie admitted. She glanced across the yard, but I didn't. I had a feeling he was still watching us. If we both looked, he'd know we were talking about him.

"He's okay, I guess." Carrie was opening the screen door that led to the front hallway. "He's kind of quiet, never says much."

I couldn't resist looking back after all, and as I followed Carrie into the house I glanced sideways, trying to seem casual. Max was still standing watching us across the yard. The rake was motionless in his hand. He wasn't even pretending *not* to watch. He was openly, deliberately staring at me . . . and it made my skin prickly. *Oh, it's just this whole place!* I thought with impatience. I didn't want to come, and the ravine made me nervous . . . and it was so dark and gloomy . . . and now this man was staring at me . . . or Carrie . . . or both of us. It didn't matter, it was creepy, whomever he was staring at.

Even when I closed the door and stood safely in Aunt Lorna's beautiful entry hall, in my mind I could still see Max standing there, silent and staring, holding the rake.

"You're home, I see." Mom was just coming down the stairway, cheerful and smiling, as though there was nothing wrong at all.

CHAPTER
SEVEN

The next morning the skies began to clear. By mid-morning a flicker of sunlight crept across the lawns around Aunt Lorna's house. The grass was dappled with light between the apple trees, and birds fluttered and splashed in the birdbath in the side yard.

Pearl came. It was Friday, her day to clean. She was polishing silver in the kitchen when Carrie and I raided the refrigerator for a before-lunch rootbeer.

Even with the sunshine, the house was still gloomy to me, with its high-ceilinged rooms and shadowy corners. And I couldn't forget how Max had stood staring after Carrie and me as we came from the woods and went into the house the afternoon before. I was glad he wasn't around this morning. Maybe it was his day off.

But it wasn't his day off. After lunch I saw him on a long ladder cleaning out gutters clogged with wet leaves. I had gone upstairs after lunch to change into a different pair of shoes, and I just happened to glance out of my window and saw Max. He didn't see me, and it was my turn to stare at him.

He was working quite close to my window, his head down, his face mostly hidden by the angle of the cap he wore. As he moved, I could occasionally see the lower part of his face. His mouth had a hard set to it, like he was mad about something. *Mad about having to clean out the messy old gutters*, I thought, trying to joke myself out of my uneasy feelings.

The sleeves of his gray work shirt were rolled to the elbows, and his arms were covered with dark freckles.

I was only a few feet away, but he didn't know I was there at my window. I hardly dared breathe as I watched him scraping out the gutter. Normally I wouldn't have spied on someone like that. *Serves you right*, I thought, *for giving me the creeps yesterday by staring at me.*

I heard the phone ringing, and then I heard Carrie's voice as she called from downstairs.

"Phone for you, Elizabeth."

Through my screened window, Max had heard Carrie's voice too. His head jerked up, and I dodged back out of sight so quickly I nearly fell over the table behind me.

How awful if he should have seen me staring at him!

I wondered if he had.

"You can take it in Mom's room," Carrie called.

I knew Max could hear her as well as I was hearing her. I didn't want to call back, "Thanks, Carrie," because I knew Max would hear that too, and realize how close I'd been to him as he worked.

So I didn't answer. I just hurried out into the hallway and down to Aunt Lorna's room.

The phone was on a table by her bed, and I perched on the edge of a chair with a green cushion that was at one side of the table.

It was only as I reached to lift the receiver that the realization came to me that someone was calling me *here*. I wasn't home in Elmwood, where Ginny and Laurene and other kids might call. I was far away in a strange town, and someone was phoning me. There was only one person I knew in Rowenville . . . oh, if only this could be him calling!

"Hi — is that you, Elizabeth?"

It *was* Greg. I felt my cheeks flush. My voice didn't sound very steady when I answered, but he didn't seem to notice.

"Yes, this is Elizabeth."

His phone voice was just as warm and friendly, full of ease and confidence, as he was in person.

"How about some of the great fried shrimp

they serve at the Blue Moon Inn tonight —
and maybe a movie afterward?"

Nothing had ever sounded better!

I hung up the phone and sat for a few
moments longer in Aunt Lorna's green chair,
thinking of all the things I should do before
seven o'clock.

Wash and blow dry my hair.

Polish my fingernails.

Not eat anything, so I would look thin.

Decide what to wear.

Oh, what if Ginny knew, I couldn't help
thinking. Greg was so nice, and good-looking,
and he was already in college. Ginny's eyes
would open wide as saucers.

And Laurene, what if Laurene knew! I
wanted to call Elmwood and spread the word.

Almost right away I forgot about Ginny
and Laurene, and all the other kids back in
Elmwood. All I thought about was Greg
Preston. Around me the house was beautiful
again, peaceful and serene in the early afternoon sunshine. There was a gentleness in the
green shadows on the lawn and the stir of a
curtain at the window. It was a beautiful,
wonderful summer afternoon, and I felt very
happy for the first time since I had arrived
at Aunt Lorna's.

My next thought was to tell Carrie. She
would remember meeting Greg when we
parked the car. We'd go to my room and look

through my clothes and decide what I should wear for this wonderful date.

I ran out of Aunt Lorna's room and along the hall to the stairway. I was just starting down, just about to call out, "Carrie —" when I felt something like a hard bar shoving against the middle of my back. I lost my balance and staggered on the stairs, clutching at the banister as I fell, twisting my ankle, stumbling to my knees.

I was halfway down the stairs before I could stop myself, bruising my fingers as I grasped for a hold on the spindles of the banister. My left ankle hurt and my left wrist throbbed with pain. Everything inside me felt jolted out of place. Even my breath had been knocked out of me. I tried to suck in air, holding the stair railing like a drowning man holds on to a helpful hand.

No one came running to help me. The house, both above and below, was undisturbed. No one knew I had fallen. The stairs were carpeted, and I hadn't screamed as I fell.

I wanted to cry out now, cry out for help, but I could barely get my breath and I felt too shaken and frightened to cry out loud enough for anyone to hear.

I looked back up the stairs, but there was nothing to see.

Then I heard Carrie's voice in the living

room. She said something and I heard Mom laugh.

Trembling, breathing with difficulty, I managed to get to my feet. I felt dizzy, and I thought how surprised everybody would be when I came limping into the living room and told them I had fallen down the stairs.

Cautiously, hugging the banister and not putting much weight on my left ankle, I edged my way carefully down the remaining stairs. I was nearly to the bottom when something warned me to turn around — a faint sound I couldn't even identify or even be sure I heard, but my impulse was to turn around. I looked behind me, back up the stairs, and out of the emptiness above me, the cane-back hall chair came hurtling down, straight toward me, tilted back so the four chair legs came at me like ramrods.

I shrank against the banister as the chair plummeted past and crashed across the floor of the entryway below, coming to rest against the frame of the living room doorway.

CHAPTER EIGHT

The sound of the chair slamming against the living room doorway instantly silenced the voices in the living room.

Then everyone came running out to see what had happened. Carrie was first, closely followed by Mom and Aunt Lorna — who was still carrying a teacup.

I'll never forget how surprised she looked, holding her teacup, gazing at a chair from the upstairs hall lying in the downstairs entryway — *for the second time*. Aunt Lorna was not prepared for disturbances like this in her happy life in Rowenville.

"Elizabeth!" Mom was the first to catch sight of me, crumpled at the foot of the stairs. She rushed over and knelt beside me and put her hands on my arm.

"Elizabeth! Honey, are you all right? What happened?"

Carrie came running toward the stairs too,

and over Mom's shoulder our eyes met. The chair had come down the stairs chasing Carrie once, and now it had come down after me. And we both knew that, as our eyes met and Mom was asking, "Elizabeth, are you hurt? Can you get up?"

Aunt Lorna came toward me as though in a daze. She stared at me and then turned to look back at the chair lying on its side by the living room doorway.

"That's the chair from the upstairs hall," she said, as Mom helped me to my feet. I was wobbly, but my ankle didn't hurt too much. My wrist hurt more, where I had wrenched my arm trying to hang onto the banister as I fell.

"Come in the living room," Aunt Lorna said, hovering with concern. "Can you walk?"

She looked so distressed I wanted to say, "Don't worry, Aunt Lorna, I'm okay." But I didn't feel okay. I didn't even feel like saying anything. I felt like something had turned me upside down and shaken me and nothing was back in the right place yet.

Leaning on Mom's arm I limped into the living room and Mom settled me on the sofa by the fireplace where green plants and flowers from the garden were arranged on the hearth. Carrie was hanging over me with a distracted look, and finally, as I sank back on the sofa cushions, she burst out: "Mother, it's happening again — don't you remember when I told you the chair sort of 'came after me' down the stairs that day — and you said it probably got put too close to the stairs when Pearl was vacuuming the hall, and just fell down by accident!"

Aunt Lorna looked more distressed than ever. She was still holding the teacup, long forgotten in her slender fingers.

"It couldn't happen twice that way," Carrie declared. "Pearl wouldn't leave it so close to the stairs *twice* — that's too much of a coincidence."

Before Aunt Lorna could answer, a protesting voice came from the living room doorway.

"Mrs. Thatcher, I didn't leave the chair by the stairs."

Pearl stood just inside the living room, looking back and forth from face to face. The commotion in the hall brought her from the kitchen, and she heard what Carrie said.

Pearl was somewhere between Mom and me in age. She had frizzy blond hair, and her plump face was set with a fretful determination to prove her innocence.

"When I vacuum the hall —" she turned and looked over her shoulder toward the stairway and the upper hall, "I always put the chair back in the right place."

I believed Pearl. I knew the chair had been a long way from the top of the stairs. Yet I felt *attacked* by the chair. As I looked at it, lying in the hallway, I could feel the hard press of a bar — the edge of the chair — against my back before I fell.

Mom sat beside me on the sofa. "Are you all right, honey?" she asked in that way moms have. I knew I'd given her a scare. I thought how I'd feel if it was the other way around and I came out of the living room and saw Mom all huddled and hurt at the foot of the stairs.

"Sure, Mom, I'm fine."

It wasn't easy to say, because my ankle and wrist hurt, and I was scared. I felt anything but fine. I wanted to talk to Carrie someplace where we could be alone. I wanted to tell her the chair had come after me down the stairs, just like it had come after her. I also wanted to tell her it had pushed me first. It had pushed me, and then after I fell, as I started to get to my feet, the chair had come after me with a terrible rush down the stairway . . . flying past me . . . slamming against the living room doorway.

"I always put the chair back in its place," Pearl said again.

No one seemed to know what else to say for the moment.

Through the living room window I could see Max, finished with the gutters, clipping the hedge at the front of the yard. A car went by on Green Oak Lane, heading into town.

Sunlight lay across the grass of Aunt Lorna's yard.

"Mother —" Carrie began, but Aunt Lorna lifted a hand to stop her.

"Not now," she said in a weary voice. "I don't want to hear anything right now about this house being haunted."

Pearl looked startled at Aunt Lorna's words, and Carrie sighed dramatically at being shushed. I sat rubbing my wrist, sympathizing with Carrie. I didn't want to upset Aunt Lorna, but I couldn't help wondering how she'd feel if she stood at the top of a stairway and felt a chair pushing against her back.

By and by Pearl went back to the kitchen and Carrie helped me upstairs to my room to rest for my date with Greg. Somewhere during all the fuss, I had managed to mention that I was supposed to go on a date with Greg Preston at seven that night.

CHAPTER
NINE

I thought about Greg Preston as I lay resting in my room. I had the whole afternoon to recuperate before he arrived at seven.

Carrie had drawn the shades part-way down, so the room was dim and restful but fresh air could come in through the bottom part of the windows. It seemed odd to be in this quiet, twilight place in the middle of a summer afternoon. I couldn't hear anything from downstairs, no voice or footstep or closing door; it was as if I was alone in the house, in the half light of the lowered shades. Even my thoughts about Greg and my anticipation of our date couldn't put me completely at ease or take my mind off the silent house around me.

I felt a sense of sadness, a sense of loss, because my original pleasure in the house had been taken from me.

As I rested with closed eyes in my dusky

room, the summer world outside gave way in my imagination to the snowy world of that wonderful Christmas visit.

On the day after Christmas, we all drove out along Green Oak Road, through the woods, to a charming, old-fashioned restaurant named the Blue Moon Inn — the same one Greg was taking me to tonight. It appeared suddenly around a bend in the road, nestled in a clearing and looking very much like merrie-olde-England with a cobbled courtyard and a large painted sign that swung in the wind.

"They have the best food you've ever tasted," Aunt Lorna promised us, as we sat consulting menus at a round oak table by a warm fireplace. A huge black iron kettle was on the hearth, and on the walls decorative brass and copper plates shone like sun in the firelight.

It *was* a delicious meal. Aunt Lorna was right about the food. The whole inn room was so cozy we lingered a long time, talking and enjoying the charm of the room and the bright fire in the fireplace.

A very handsome young man with dark curly hair and sideburns came to the table to ask if we had enjoyed our meal. He had on a dark suit and dark tie with a gold tiepin. He seemed eager to please, and he said he was glad we liked the food. Carrie and I exchanged silent "look-at-*him*" glances across the table. When he moved off, we saw him stop to chat at another table, and Aunt Lorna said in an undertone, "I think he's the new manager."

Whoever he was, he sure was handsome! Carrie and I wished he'd come to our table again, but he didn't.

Dad was driving, and as we left the Blue Moon Inn, Aunt Lorna asked him to go on farther along the road through the woods.

"It's only another couple of miles, and there's something I think you'd like to see," she said, especially to Mom. "Remember when we were little and they used to freeze the playground at Wilson Park for skating?"

"Of course I remember!" Mom said. "What fun we had there!"

I watched through the car windows as the wintry woods passed by. The trees held out snow-lined branches, as though for my inspection. Occasionally I caught sight of a dark-winged bird against the pale December sky.

The place Aunt Lorna wanted us to see was a large pond, frozen over now with rough gray ice. An unpainted wooden shack stood at one end of the pond. The door was gone and the two small windows were broken and edged with grimy shards.

"In Rowenville they flood the vacant lot behind the Fire Department for skating nowadays," Aunt Lorna said, as we opened car doors and stepped out into the snowy woods by the frozen pond. "So the town children don't come here anymore. But isn't it interesting — come and look —" She started toward the old shack.

We followed after her, Dad with his hands in his overcoat pocket because he'd forgotten his gloves in the car.

"Marian brought me here once," Aunt Lorna explained, referring to the friend who had found the house on Green Oak Lane. "This was the warming house for the skaters."

Carrie and I were close behind Aunt Lorna and Mom as they peered into the darkness of the abandoned shack. Then Aunt Lorna stepped inside and we followed. There was a long bench on each wall, where the children had sat to put on their skates, tucking their shoes and boots under the bench. The light was poor, but an old pot-bellied stove, rusted and layered with dust, was visible in the middle of the room.

"Yes, this is interesting," Mom said, turning her head to look around at the crude benches and rough walls.

I touched the old stove gingerly. Once upon a time it had been clean and new, too hot to touch as I was touching it now. There would have been a warm fire inside. Once upon a time children sat on the benches struggling with skate laces, stumping in and out from the icy pond to the warmth of the stove. Parents watched from the banks of the pond, or sat on a bench in the warming house, talking and waiting to drive their children back to town again.

"I bet it was fun here," Carrie said.

"I'm sure it was." Aunt Lorna nodded. "Marian said it hasn't been used in years, but she remembers coming here to skate when she was a little girl."

We came outside again, and Aunt Lorna motioned to the pond with its close encircling of trees. "This is a beautiful picnic spot in the summertime, and also" — she laughed a little — "also sort of a lovers' rendezvous, I've heard, here by the pond under the trees."

"I think it's a little too cold for romance right now," Dad said, and we were all glad to get back in the warm car.

I looked at the pond a last time as we drove away, and I could imagine I saw children skating on the frozen surface and smoke rising from the chimney of the warming house.

Echoes of voices long gone followed me as our car sped away, back along Green Oak Road toward town.

The light was fading as we pulled into the driveway beside Aunt Lorna's house that afternoon. December days were short, and by four-thirty twilight had come. It had been a wonderful afternoon. Everything at Aunt

Lorna's house was wonderful then. Dad stretched out his legs and basked in the warmth of the log fire in the living room. Carrie turned on the Christmas tree lights and Aunt Lorna made eggnog, thick and sweet and sprinkled with dark grains of nutmeg that floated on top.

We were all very happy.

CHAPTER
TEN

It was the second day after Christmas that things had stopped being quite so happy . . . and there was more to come that we didn't even dream of then.

Now I lay on the bed, remembering, moving my wrist cautiously to see if it still moved okay. It hurt, but it moved. My ankle felt almost normal. The breeze had faded away at the windows and the room was warm. I felt drowsy, half asleep and half awake . . . recalling that second day after Christmas . . . remembering Carrie's bright face, the face of a girl in love.

"Tom will drive us home, Mom," Carrie said. *"We'll meet him at the coffee shop and he'll drive us home."*

Tom was the first boyfriend Carrie had ever had. She was usually very shy with boys, and I was surprised when she wrote to me about Tom, just a few weeks after she started going to Rowenville High.

She had written to me about him in the fall. By the time the school had its Winter Dance, early in December, Carrie and Tom were going steady. A jumble of memories came to my mind . . . Carrie's letters, scribbled and exuberant . . . a slightly out-of-focus photo of the wonderful Tom Abbott standing by a car . . . another photo of Carrie and Tom at the Winter Dance, smiling self-consciously, a reflection of flashbulbs glistening in the background.

Amid this jumble of memories, the particular memory of that second day after Christmas kept coming back.

"Tom will drive us home, Mom. We'll meet him at the coffee shop and he'll drive us home. No problem."

Wrong.

There was a "problem." Her name was Bonnie Vayle.

It was Christmas money that took us shopping in Rowenville that day, Carrie and me. Aunt Estelle, who lived in California (and thought everyone else should too) had sent us each a twenty-five dollar check for Christmas.

"And it's burning a hole in your pockets,"

Dad said as he let us out of the car on Rowen Avenue to do our shopping.

Dad and Mom and Aunt Lorna were going on to some antique shops in a nearby town, then to dinner with Aunt Lorna's friend Marian Weatherby. Carrie and I were going to buy great things like sweaters and lipsticks, whatever we wanted, whatever twenty-five dollars would buy. Then we were going to the Minuette to have something to eat and meet Tom. A few snowflakes fell through the cold afternoon as we stood on the sidewalk by the stores and waved goodbye to Mom and Dad and Aunt Lorna. It was about three o'clock.

When the car was gone, Carrie and I went up Rowen Avenue, feeling wealthy and extravagant.

It was after five when we got to the Minuette. Tom Abbott was already there, sitting on a stool at the counter. He got up from the counter and went with us to a booth by the window that looked out on Rowen Avenue. It was already dark. The snow had stopped and a chill of falling temperatures filled the air.

I had never been in the Minuette before, but I had been in places like it; a counter with swivel stools and plastic domes over plates of donuts, booths by the windows, a few small tables, a casual air of camaraderie between customers and waitresses. Strings of colored Christmas lights around the windows for the holidays created a bright, festive atmosphere.

On our booth-table there was a metal container for paper napkins and a sugar bowl. Tom had brought along the cup of coffee he was drinking, and he pulled a paper napkin from the container to blot coffee that had spilled into the saucer.

I had met Tom on Christmas Day, when he came by Aunt Lorna's to see Carrie. He had a slender face, with dark eyes and a rather romantic look. There was a quiet politeness about him, and I had noticed that when you talked to him he really listened. I liked him and I thought he was just right for Carrie.

"Look what I bought." Carrie opened her bag from Rowen Boutique and took out the sweater she had bought after trying on umpteen other sweaters.

"And this." While Tom was still admiring the sweater, Carrie took a gold bracelet from another bag.

Of course it wasn't *real* gold. But it had a lovely golden sheen and when Carrie pushed it on her wrist it looked great.

"Show him what *you* bought, Elizabeth," Carrie said. She leaned across the booth toward me, and just at that moment I was aware of someone sliding into the empty space beside me, mimicking Carrie's words.

"Yes, show us all what *you* bought, Elizabeth." The words were friendly.

It was Bonnie Vayle — although I didn't know her name then. All I knew was that a pretty, yellow-haired girl in a blue jacket had sat down beside me in the booth.

Carrie introduced us, and I had the feeling that Carrie hoped Bonnie wouldn't stay too long.

But she stayed and stayed. She stayed while Carrie and I ordered chili dogs and fries, and she told the waitress she would only have a Coke because she had to eat dinner with her family when she got home.

She stayed on while Carrie and I ate our chili dogs, and I wished I hadn't ordered something so messy to eat. Bonnie Vayle looked glamorous and nonchalant sipping her Coke, while I spilled chili on my fingers and used up half the napkins in the metal container.

Since Tom was only drinking coffee and Bonnie was only drinking her Coke, they did most of the talking. Carrie and I had to eat, once we'd ordered. But it was horrible to spill chili and eat French fries and get my fingers greasy while the girl next to me looked like a magazine cover. Carrie lost interest in her food too, about the third time Bonnie told Tom how wonderful he was.

Bonnie and Tom were both seniors, and they had several classes together. "You always know what to say when Mr. Robbins calls on you," Bonnie insisted, as Tom shook his head modestly. "Yes you do, Tommy. You're the smartest one in the class."

It didn't take much to see that Tom was beginning to think he was as wonderful as Bonnie said he was. She was probably one of the "popular" senior-class girls and Tom was flattered by all her attention. He sort of forgot for the moment about Carrie, sitting beside him with a plate of food growing cold.

A waitress came to fill Tom's coffee cup. Bonnie joked with her about something and I could see they were friends. But I didn't pay too much attention to the waitress; I was beginning to feel sorry for Carrie — and annoyed with Bonnie and Tom.

Carrie, who hadn't been saying much to begin with, grew completely silent. And I couldn't think of anything to say, I didn't go to Rowenville High. I didn't know the teachers they were talking about or the kids or anything about the school affairs.

The conversation was all Bonnie's and Tom's.

The waitress came back to see if Carrie and I wanted dessert, and before we could answer, Tom said to Carrie, "What's it going to be, the diet or dessert?"

He finally remembered she was there, and he had to say something like that! I could see Carrie stiffen, and I knew how embarrassed she was. She might have confided to Tom about trying to lose weight, but she certainly didn't want to discuss it in front of Bonnie Vayle — who was thin, of course.

Before I even had a chance to hope the whole conversation would be dropped, Bonnie smiled across the booth at Carrie smugly. "You're on a diet?" she said, stroking a strand of her yellow hair. "No dessert for you."

"Carrie would rather have two dips of chocolate ice cream," Tom said, all smiles for Bonnie again.

Bonnie shook her finger at Carrie. "I don't know if I would do that," she said, barely smiling. The waitress was smiling too. Everybody was happy except Carrie — and me. I wanted to give Tom a kick under the table, for what good that would have done.

"She'll have the ice cream," Tom told the waitress without waiting for Carrie to make up her own mind.

"I'll have ice cream too," I said loyally. The waitress scurried off, and Bonnie stroked her hair again. "I never eat ice cream," she said.

"I eat it all the time," I said, while Carrie sat with downcast eyes, intimidated by Bonnie's presence and Tom's *dumb* behavior.

To make matters worse, when Bonnie decided it was time to go home (finally) and said she didn't have her car with her, Tom jumped right up and said he'd drive her home.

"Oh, would you, Tommy — that's great!" She stood by the booth knotting a scarf jauntily around her neck and looking like a movie star.

The waitress had just set down dishes of ice cream for Carrie and me, and Bonnie said, "You can take me home while they have their ice cream."

I could already see her snuggling up to Tom in the car . . . "Ooohh, it's so cold, Tommy," she'd say — something like that.

Tom was fumbling in his pocket for his car keys.

"Listen, Carrie — I'll be right back —"

But Carrie was shaking her head. "We have a ride," she said.

I looked across the booth at Carrie with surprise. What ride did we have?

"You've got a ride?" Tom was surprised too. "I thought you said —"

"That's all changed," Carrie interrupted. Her voice sounded thin and unnatural. "You go ahead with Bonnie. My mom's coming for us."

"That's nice," Bonnie said. She looked at Tom. "Are we ready, Tommy?"

Tom shrugged. "I guess so," he said. "I'll call you in the morning, Carrie." I watched as he left the Minuette with Bonnie hanging on his arm. A cold blast of air shot through the restaurant when they opened the door to go outside. I didn't want to be out in that cold, and I wondered what ride Carrie had lined up for us.

"Carrie?" I looked across the booth and saw tears glistening in her eyes.

I knew she was angry and hurt that Bonnie had flirted with Tom, and that Tom had been so taken in.

We sat silently for a few more minutes. Neither one of us wanted to eat the ice cream, but I took a few bites and pushed the rest around with my spoon. Finally I tried again. "Carrie? About that ride?"

She lifted her head and looked at me across the booth. Her eyes were shimmering with tears, and her mouth was drawn tight.

"I'd rather walk home through the snow in my bare feet than let Tom Abbott drive me."

We went up to the cash register at the front counter to pay our bill. A short, pudgy man sat there; I suppose he was the owner of the Minuette.

Carrie buttoned her coat, tugged gloves out of her pocket.

As we opened the door, I pulled up the hood of my jacket. It was a lousy, cold, miserable night. The wind hit us as soon as we stepped out to the street. It was well after six o'clock now, and the stores along Rowen Avenue were closed. Dark display windows lined the cold, windy street we had to walk.

"Carrie — let's call home," I begged as we set off, heads down against the wind.

"Nobody's at home."

We passed another darkened store window. The wind was dreadful, and I felt anything was worth a try.

"Maybe they're home — maybe they had an early dinner and they're home — let's at least try."

I had hopeful visions of Mom and Dad and Aunt Lorna sitting warm and comfortable around the fireplace in Aunt Lorna's living room after an early dinner. Just waiting for us to call.

Carrie looked at me with a worn expression.

"Elizabeth, they're not home." Her voice was weary, but I clung to her arm and tried again. "Let's at least call, Carrie."

At the next corner there was a drugstore, and we went inside. The world came at once to order; warm, secure; aisles of shampoo, face cream, cold remedies. I followed Carrie back toward the phone booth.

Past a girl in a blue smock at the make-up counter.

Past paperback books, vitamins, camera supplies.

Carrie dialed the number, while I stood outside the phone booth, listening.

I watched Carrie's face. The phone was ringing, but nobody was answering. Nobody was at home.

Carrie hung up the receiver and stood looking at me. Wisps of hair draggled on her forehead and her dark eyes were sad.

"Call a cab," I said, and she laughed. "Elizabeth, there isn't any cab service in Rowenville."

She pushed past me, out of the phone booth, and we went back through the brightly lit drugstore.

Outside on Rowen Avenue the night seemed more desolate than ever. Even Carrie looked daunted. "I don't care," she insisted bleakly. "Tom Abbott can drive Bonnie home if he wants to. I don't care."

But I cared. I trudged after Carrie along Rowen Avenue, which was bad enough. But then we turned onto Green Oak Lane. The wind had risen and it was beginning to snow again. Cold, stinging snowflakes hit our faces.

"Carrie, this is crazy —" I felt my voice muffled by the hood I was trying to hold closer around my face.

Carrie didn't answer, trudging on beside me through the snow. I didn't try to talk after that.

I knew she had started out with some grim

sense of satisfaction, but the satisfaction was rapidly fading away as we marched on.

The wind was strong, and bitter cold. We leaned into it, heads down. We wanted to be home. Tears stung our eyes. All the houses we passed were like houses in a dream — lighted windows far away through the snow.

I looked sideways at Carrie. Her face was drooping; all the spirited determination when she spoke to Tom at the coffee shop was gone.

I had never been so cold in my life.

Green Oak Lane stretched on forever ahead of us. There was no end.

I thought we would *never* get to Aunt Lorna's house.

And I hated Bonnie Vayle and Tom Abbott. They were safe somewhere, I thought; they were safe somewhere in Tom's warm car. And Bonnie Vayle was saying, "Thanks, Tommy, thanks for the ride home."

After a long, *long* time we saw Aunt Lorna's house. We saw the snow-covered hedges and gardens and the driveway that led to the front door. We were stumbling then, after the long walk. My feet were numb, my face aching with cold. We had walked all the way from Rowen Avenue. Nearly two miles in the cold wind and snow.

The house stood ahead of us, dark, silhouetted against the snowy sky.

Carrie ran up the steps and pulled a key from her purse.

The entry hall was empty, a lamp burning on the table. The rest of the house was dark, silent; Mom and Dad and Aunt Lorna were still away.

Carrie ran toward the stairs in tears, and I stood in the entry, feeling Aunt Lorna's house close in around me, dark and mournful.

Darn Bonnie Vayle, I thought. And darn Tom Abbott for believing all her flattery and jumping up so quickly to drive her home.

CHAPTER
ELEVEN

As we had set off dramatically from the Minuette — Carrie hurt and defiant, me thinking about how cold it was and how far away Aunt Lorna's house was — we forgot one of our packages. The bag that contained Carrie's new sweater was found in the corner of the booth after we left. When Carrie missed it the next morning and we called the Minuette, the man who answered the phone assured us the package was safe in the Lost-and-Found drawer.

We didn't dash right off to get the sweater. Tom had said he'd call Carrie in the morning, and I knew she was waiting for his call. Someone had given Aunt Lorna a five-hundred-piece jigsaw puzzle for Christmas, and we spread it out on a large table in the living room. Everyone took a turn working at it off and on between breakfast and lunch — Aunt Lorna, Mom; even Dad tried.

91

"There are too many blue pieces," he protested at last, pushing back his chair. "Come on, Elizabeth, your turn again."

It was a strange morning. I felt the time going by somewhere in the distance, like faint background music that no one was listening to. We talked and worked on the puzzle and everything was normal on the surface; but somewhere time was going by and I knew Carrie was straining her ears for the sound of the phone ringing when Tom called. And I realized that I was too.

As the hours passed and there was no call, I reminded myself that boys weren't always as precise as girls wanted them to be. He'd probably call at two in the afternoon — close enough to morning in his estimation. Maybe he didn't even remember that he had said "morning."

Of course on the other hand there was always the possibility that Tom had fallen wildly in love with Bonnie Vayle when he drove her home, and didn't know how to call Carrie and break the news to her.

I thought of everything, as the morning went by.

We had salmon salad for lunch, and Carrie and I washed the dishes afterward. She looked so sad and wistful I couldn't help saying one more time, "Don't worry, he'll call. Everything will be all right."

She looked at me wanly, wanting to believe what I said. But she couldn't.

"Oh, Elizabeth, what if he never ever calls me again?"

Her voice wavered, as she lifted the dishes mechanically and put them into the soapy water.

"That's just plain silly," I told her. I tried to sound as confident as I could, which was more confident than I felt. What if Tom really had fallen in love with Bonnie? What if the whole day went by and he never did call?

"He got busy with something," I said. "You know how boys are. He'll be calling any minute."

We finished the dishes in silence, but the phone didn't ring.

Carrie emptied the dishwater and dried her hands on a towel.

"I'm not waiting around here all afternoon," she said. "Let's go and get my sweater."

It looked cold as the North Pole outside. It was a perfect day to stay indoors by the fire and work the Christmas jigsaw puzzle and eat Christmas cookies. But I said, "Sure, that's a good idea. Let's get your sweater."

We bundled up in boots and mufflers and good warm coats, and Aunt Lorna gave us a grocery list. "As long as you're going out," she said.

The snow had stopped and the wind was gone, but it was still freezing cold. Carrie and I sat in the garage for a few minutes letting the car warm up before we started out, right straight back along the road that had seemed so endless the night before.

When we got to the Minuette, a waitress behind the counter recognized Carrie right away. She waved to us and disappeared through a door marked "Private" to get Carrie's sweater.

"That's Bonnie's girlfriend Janette," Carrie said. "She works here part-time. You remember her from last night."

I nodded vaguely, which was just about the way I remembered the waitress. My memories of the night before were mostly about Bonnie and Tom and walking home in the cold.

After Janette brought the sweater from the Lost-and-Found, we decided to stay and have some tea. I knew Carrie didn't want to go right back home and start listening for a phone that wasn't ringing.

It was not a busy hour of the day at the coffee shop. A few customers came and went. At a booth near ours two elderly gentlemen had opened a checkerboard and I heard Janette teasing them as she went by.

"No cheating now, Mr. Amos!"

Janette was short and a little plump, with

black curly hair and a perky smile. I thought she would have her share of boyfriends, even if she wasn't as beautiful as her friend Bonnie.

I couldn't remember anything else about the Minuette that afternoon. I knew now that Greg Preston had been there and seen me while I sat drinking tea with Carrie. But I didn't see him. I soon forgot to notice anything, as Carrie and I got to talking about Bonnie.

As I thought back about what we did while we drank our tea it seemed incredibly silly. But it hadn't seemed silly at the time. It seemed like just the right thing to do: We decided to get even with Bonnie for flirting with Tom.

"It's all her fault we had to walk home in the cold," Carrie said glumly. "You *know* it was all her fault. She just made me so mad I had to do *something*."

"Sure. I understand." I stirred my tea and smiled at Carrie. If I tried hard maybe in a couple of hundred years I could forget how cold and miserable that walk home had been. And maybe if I had a nice boyfriend like Tom and a girl like Bonnie flirted with him and he offered to drive her home, I'd have done the same thing Carrie did.

"She only lives a couple of blocks away," Carrie said. "She could have walked home."

"Tom didn't think so."

It was a poor joke, and Carrie didn't laugh.

"Maybe I just won't bother to talk to Tom right away when he calls," Carrie said, trying to sound staunch and firm. Tom hadn't called at all yet, but we both ignored that fact.

"That's a good idea," I said. "I'll tell him you're too busy to come to the phone. Or maybe I could even say you're not home. I could sound a little nervous, like I don't want to give away that you're out with another boy."

"Do you think you could do that?" Carrie looked at me doubtfully. "I mean, could you get him to think I'm out with another boy just by the way you say I'm not home?"

"Oh, sure." I made it sound like I did this all the time. I cleared my throat and said mysteriously, "Hello, Tom. I'm *so sorry* Carrie isn't here — well, that is, she isn't here right *now* — but of course she'll be back — well, ummm, *soon*, sometime soon." I paused for Carrie's reaction. "How does that sound?"

"Not bad." Carrie even laughed a little. I was glad her sense of humor was returning. But she grew silent again almost right away, and pushed her teaspoon back and forth aimlessly. It was really Bonnie Vayle she held to blame, for flirting with Tom in the first place.

"Does Bonnie go steady with anyone?" I asked, just out of curiosity.

Carrie shook her head. "She has lots of boyfriends. She used to go steady with a boy on the basketball team last year, but she's not going steady with anyone this year."

I thought about that for a few moments. Then I said, just kidding, "What Bonnie needs is her own steady boyfriend, so she'll leave other girls' boyfriends alone."

"Amen," Carrie said.

And somehow that started it, gave us our idea about getting even with Bonnie. We decided if she didn't have her own steady boyfriend we would give her a "secret admirer" to take her mind off Tom.

Her secret admirer would write her a note and tell her how crazy he was about her, and that would take her mind off Tom for a while.

"Have you got some paper?" I had a pencil, and Carrie found a small spiral notebook in her purse. She tore out a blank page.

She pushed the paper across the tabletop toward me. "What are you going to write?"

"Dear Bonnie, I'm crazy about you — something like that. Oh, no — this is better!"

Meet me at the old skating pond at four o'clock.

I printed neatly, saying the words aloud as I wrote.

Aunt Lorna said the pond was a popular place for picnics and dates, so Bonnie would know where it was.

"Oh, Elizabeth, that's great!" Carrie's eyes sparkled with mischief. We were not only giving Bonnie a secret admirer, but sending her on a wild goose chase at the same time. It was perfect!

"You sign it," I said, pushing the piece of paper back toward Carrie. "Then it will be from both of us."

Carrie signed the note — disguising her handwriting:

Your secret admirer.

She folded the paper and wrote Bonnie's name on the outside.

We were sure Bonnie would never pass up an opportunity to meet a secret admirer.

How clever we thought we were. There was no one at the cash register, and Janette was watching the checker game. Nobody noticed as we walked by the counter and furtively tucked the note for Bonnie under a napkin holder.

Sometime after we were gone, Janette would find the note when she was waiting on a customer or wiping off the counter. With various people in and out all afternoon she would never know who had left it.

The only thing to wonder about was whether Bonnie would come into the coffee shop to get her note. Even though Carrie said Bonnie was in there all the time, maybe today she wouldn't come.

We braced ourselves against the cold as we went out onto Rowen Avenue. There was a grocery store just down the block and we ran along, laughing about our joke on Bonnie.

"How long do you think she'll wait for her secret admirer?" Carrie smiled.

We got a cart at the entryway of the grocery and trundled it along the aisles. Milk. Lettuce. Cheddar cheese. Bananas. Kleenex. We didn't think Aunt Lorna's grocery list was very exciting, so we added a package of cornmeal tortillas. Tomorrow we would have tacos for lunch. Enough with salmon salad.

We had to face the cold again as we came out of the grocery. A wind was rising. At least we had the car this time, I thought; we didn't have to walk home like we had the night before! We hurried back toward the car, parked across the street from the Minuette. I held the bag of groceries while Carrie bent to put the key in the car door.

"Remember," Carrie looked up at me as she turned the key, dark hair blowing around her face, "it's our secret. We'll never tell anyone."

"Our secret," I said.

I meant it. We both meant it. It was our secret. We would never tell. Bonnie Vayle could ask us a thousand questions, but we would never tell. We giggled. Maybe Bonnie Vayle would wait hours and hours for her secret admirer who didn't even exist.

"Oh, she probably won't even get the note," Carrie said, growing serious as the car door swung open.

I was about to say probably she wouldn't, when we saw Bonnie's car drive up in front of the Minuette. It was a bright red car with non-matching hubcaps and a dented rear fender, but it was her own. She hopped out and hurried into the coffee shop without a glance in our direction. We stood staring with amazement at the narrow margin of time — we had only been at the grocery a few minutes — and at how quickly our question about Bonnie coming to the coffee shop had been answered.

Carrie looked at me with a rather surprised expression, but I winked back mischievously. Now Bonnie would get her note, and at four o'clock she would make a pointless trip out to the old skating pond and the abandoned warming house to meet her non-existent admirer.

"Our secret," I reminded Carrie. "What can we lose? Come on, let's get in, I'm freezing."

We got in the car and sat for a few moments looking across the street at the coffee shop. With the dull winter light on the windows we couldn't see much inside; mostly we saw the neon sign, BEST FOOD IN TOWN.

By three o'clock that afternoon snow had started to fall again. It thickened quickly to a true snowfall, with large wet flakes coming in endless number from the gray vastness that stretched above us.

Carrie and I watched the snow from the warm comfort of the living room. Dad was upstairs and Aunt Lorna and Mom were in the kitchen, so we had the living room to ourselves. The afternoon darkened with the snowfall and Carrie turned on the Christmas tree lights. The room was beautiful, and the snowy world beyond the windows was beautiful.

But it also looked a little dangerous.

"She won't go now, with this snow," Carrie whispered, as we stood at the windows overlooking the front lawn.

I gazed at the whirling flakes. It was difficult to see very far into the distance. It would be bad driving.

"No, I guess she won't," I had to agree with Carrie.

And then it didn't seem to matter after all, whether Bonnie even got our dumb note, because just then the phone rang.

Carrie and I turned and looked at each

other, and then looked toward the living room door. From the hallway beyond we heard the next phone-ring cut off suddenly as the receiver was lifted. A moment later Aunt Lorna was at the doorway.

"Phone, Carrie."

Carrie cast a happy smile back over her shoulder, and I said, "Told you so," as she hurried out to the hall.

It was Tom, of course. He'd had to help out at his father's Photo and Office Supply Store, and this was his first opportunity to call.

There had been no cause to worry. He hadn't fallen in love with Bonnie. He'd driven her home — period. Carrie was still his girl. She came back from the phone looking dreamy and happy.

So everything was fine. Except that the next day we heard Bonnie Vayle had been killed when her car skidded off a curve a short way out of town on Green Oak Road about four o'clock in the afternoon.

CHAPTER TWELVE

I lay in the dim summer light, realizing I hadn't let myself remember that Christmas visit in such detail for a long time. Bits and pieces often flashed through my mind, but now as I lay resting in the shaded room I remembered it all in detail.

When we had heard that Bonnie Vayle was dead, Carrie had turned as pale as a ghost, but everyone thought that was because Bonnie had been a classmate. *Oh,* I thought, *there's so much more you don't know!* But they would never know. We would never tell. It was our secret, Carrie's and mine.

The rest of our Christmas stay I'd felt overwhelmed with guilt and anguish, and Aunt Lorna's house became part of all my tormented thoughts. The view from my window wasn't beautiful anymore, just cold and desolate and mournful, and I wanted to be home in Elmwood and put everything that had happened out of my mind.

I pulled myself out of the past. Home was where I wanted to be now. I sat up and looked at the clock on the bedside table. It was already after five, time to start thinking about getting ready for my date with Greg.

But I didn't get up. I lay back on the bed and closed my eyes and wished I was home, away from this house and the memories it held and the atmosphere of . . . of something wrong; that was the way Carrie had put it. Something *was* wrong — illusive and frightening; when we turned to look, no one was there. *Oh yes,* I thought wearily, *I want to go home. . . .*

I must have been exhausted, for I fell asleep; and the next thing I knew Carrie was shaking my arm gently. "Elizabeth — Elizabeth — time to get up — you haven't forgotten your date, have you?"

I had to take a fast shower and hurry with dressing, and it wasn't easy to hurry with a sore wrist. But when Greg came I was ready, sitting on the porch with Carrie and Aunt Lorna and Mom, drinking iced tea.

Max was working late. I could see him at the far end of the side yard, by the grove of apple trees. I looked the other way and tried to forget he was there.

When I saw Greg's car turn into the driveway my heart jumped. He parked and came walking toward the porch steps, looking even more handsome than I remembered him.

After the introductions were over, Greg accepted Aunt Lorna's invitation to have a glass of iced tea before we left. I had asked that we not make a big deal about my falling downstairs, so no one mentioned it. In the peaceful porch setting, with the rays of early evening sun slanting across the lawns, it was easy to put unpleasant things out of mind and I was half persuaded that nothing was really wrong at Aunt Lorna's house and that I had only imagined I felt a chair pressing itself against my back as I started down the stairs.

And then, destroying my new peace of mind, Max came across the grass and stood at the opposite side of the porch. I could see his face through the porch railings and he was staring at me as intently as he had stared the day Carrie and I came out of the woods. No one else noticed him for the moment, and I looked down into my glass of tea stupidly, wishing he would go away or stop staring — anything. And then I heard Aunt Lorna's voice, friendly, casual; "Oh, here's Max — excuse me for a moment."

She went across to the other side of the long porch and we could catch a word now and then as she gave Max instructions for transplanting some rosebushes the next morning. I noticed that Greg kept glancing over

105

toward Aunt Lorna and Max, and when Aunt Lorna came back and resumed her place among us, Greg watched as Max walked back along the driveway to his car, a dark blue Chevy, not too new-looking.

Aunt Lorna was pouring more iced tea for Mom, and Carrie retrieved a paper napkin that fluttered to the floor.

Max started his car and drove around Greg's car in the driveway. On Green Oak Lane, he turned toward town.

I was glad to see him leaving. I found myself wishing he wasn't ever coming back. I didn't like the way he looked at me, and it made me nervous to have him around . . . even as I was thinking this I heard Aunt Lorna telling Greg, "Highly recommended . . . has a green thumb."

Aunt Lorna was happy with her house and her gardener. But I wished he'd go away and never come back.

"Shall we go?" Greg touched my arm to get my attention. I guess he'd had all the iced tea and polite conversation he wanted for the time. And I was glad to go too. I wanted to be with Greg and forget all my Christmas memories, forget my fall down the stairs. As we walked toward his car I had a sense of excitement about the evening ahead. It was wonderful to be starting out on a warm summer evening, just as dusk was falling, with someone as nice as Greg.

But as I drove off with Greg, I didn't leave any problems behind me after all. We hadn't gone far when he said, "What do you think of that guy who works for your aunt?"

We were on Green Oak Road, and the woods surrounded us, drenched in the rich golden light of the day's end.

I looked at Greg uncertainly. Could I tell him something so vague, so almost foolish-sounding as "he sort of gives me the creeps"? There wasn't any real, concrete reason why I shouldn't like Max. Apparently he was an efficient gardener. Aunt Lorna was pleased with his work.

"Come on." Greg laughed at my hesitation. "You must have some opinion of him."

"He sort of gives me the creeps," I finally admitted. "I suppose that sounds silly."

"Not really." Greg's voice was sober.

We drove in silence for a few moments.

"I don't like him much myself," Greg said.

"You don't?" I couldn't help being surprised. "I didn't know you knew him."

Greg shook his head. "I don't know him. But I *have* seen him before."

We had reached the Blue Moon Inn, where already there were cars in the parking area at the side. Friday night was busy at the Blue Moon.

Greg had made a reservation, and we were taken to a table for two by a window. It was a side window, looking out on the woods.

Across the room I could see the big round table where Mom and Dad and Aunt Lorna and Carrie and I had eaten our lunch that winter day that seemed so long ago.

"Let's decide what we want," Greg suggested, as a waiter put menus on our table. "Then we can talk."

I looked at the list of foods, wondering where our conversation would lead when we continued it.

A bus boy brought glasses of water, and a few minutes later reappeared and put a basket of warm rolls on the table. The rolls grew cold while we talked.

"Do you remember I told you I'd seen you one afternoon at the Minuette?" Greg began, when the waiter had taken our order and gotten the oversized menus out of our way.

I didn't know what to say. Greg had been in the coffee shop *that* afternoon, that awful afternoon. Maybe he had heard Carrie and I composing our note to Bonnie. Maybe he would suddenly say, "I know what you did!"

But when I lifted my eyes and looked across the table he was watching me with a flirtatious expression, and I felt myself blushing.

"I remember," I said. I know my smile was self-conscious, but I couldn't help it. The conversation was taking a romantic turn.

But I was wrong. The conversation was returning to Max. Greg's next words were:

"That man who is now your aunt's gardener was in the Minuette the same afternoon I saw you there."

I had a premonition that something bad was coming, but I didn't know what. I lifted my water glass and the ice tinkled softly. The hostess was leading people to a table near ours, and I heard the soft rustle of a woman's dress as she passed.

Greg leaned toward me across the table. He lowered his voice as he continued.

"You were sitting in a booth near the back, if you remember."

I remembered.

"I was at the back end of the counter, where it curves around, so I could see out over the whole room. I saw you two there." Greg paused and smiled. "Well, I couldn't really see your cousin, her back was toward me. But I could see you, and I said to myself, 'There's a pretty girl.'"

Greg paused again and then went on. "It wasn't long before you two got up and went to the cash register to pay your check. Janette came over to the cash register and took your money and you went out. I was through about that time, so I thought I'd pay my check. There was this guy just ahead of me at the cash register, and he was staring out the window. You and your cousin were waiting to cross the street. You were standing there, and then there was a break in traffic and you ran across the street. I could still see both of you as you started walking along the other side of the street — and the man was still watching too."

We were going to the grocery store, I thought. But I didn't say anything. I just watched Greg's face, wondering what he would say next. It was weird to think that as Carrie and I went off to get Aunt Lorna's groceries, people were watching us from the Minuette window.

"The man had a funny look on his face. I didn't like it. It was kind of a mean look. Janette was at the cash register and he asked her about you and your cousin."

"He asked her about us?" I echoed the words with surprise.

Greg nodded. A waiter appeared and put salads on the table, but neither Greg nor I were ready to start eating.

"So he said, 'You know those girls?' — something like that. Janette looked out of the window to see who he was talking about. You and your cousin were across the street then, walking away."

To get Aunt Lorna's groceries, I thought.

"Janette said something about a girl from school, but she didn't know the other girl, something like that."

"She knew Carrie from school," I said. "And of course she didn't know me. I was just visiting Carrie for Christmas vacation."

Beyond the windows of the Blue Moon Inn the sun had set. Radiant streaks of crimson stretched above the woods. As we sat talking, darkness came, with deepening blue light in the sky over the woods.

"And you remembered that afternoon after all this time," I said.

"I have a good memory for faces," Greg reminded me. "I'd rather remember pretty faces like yours, but I also remember that guy's face. When he left the Minuette that day, Janette told me his name was Max. How long has he been working for your aunt?"

"Only a couple of months."

"It looks like she's satisfied with his work," Greg said thoughtfully. "But I didn't like the way he was watching you and your cousin. There's something odd about him, something I just don't trust."

When I didn't say anything right away, he added, "And now you tell me he gives you the creeps."

"He does." I answered slowly, thinking how I could best express the uneasiness that I felt when Max was around. "He makes me nervous — he stares — oh, I don't know."

I was afraid I wasn't making myself very clear. It was hard to put into words.

"I liked Joseph better," I finished lamely.

"Joseph?"

Of course Greg couldn't have known who I meant. Our food arrived, and while we ate

I told him about Aunt Lorna's first gardener, the kind, middle-aged Joseph who had fallen and died in the ravine in the woods.

The restaurant was filled to capacity. At one point, looking across the room, I saw people sitting on the chairs in the foyer, waiting for tables. The Blue Moon Inn was certainly popular. I wondered if the handsome young man who had come to our table that winter day was still around. I didn't see him in the crowded room. And except maybe to tell Carrie I hadn't seen him, I didn't care. Greg was the only one I was interested in right now.

I remembered how happy I'd been to see him coming out of the coffee shop that morning Carrie and I went to buy Tom's birthday present.

"Do you go to the Minuette a lot?" I asked. All of a sudden I thought of Janette, with her cheerful smile and curly black hair. Did Greg go there to see her?

"Every small town's got something like the Minuette, a place where everyone goes."

"And Janette's a very pretty waitress."

Greg laughed and shook his head. "No, it's nothing like that." His expression grew serious. "She's a real nice girl though, and I feel sorry for her. Her best friend was killed in an auto accident last winter."

The last thing in the world I wanted to talk about was suddenly there before me and I stared at Greg with dismay. *I don't want to talk about Bonnie Vayle.* I sent a silent message he didn't receive.

"It was a real tragedy," he continued somberly. "She was on Green Oak Road," he gestured toward the windows, "just back a mile or so. It was a bad day, bad weather conditions."

I wasn't saying anything. I felt numb. I didn't want to hear anything more about that snowy afternoon.

"Bonnie wasn't a careful driver." Greg's voice was regretful. "She was known for her fast driving. It was obviously a case of driving too fast for conditions. The road was slick with snow and she took a curve too fast."

He lifted his hands in a helpless gesture.

"What more can I say. It was a bad combination: the snow, the sharp curve, her fast driving."

A bad combination. Maybe so. Bonnie was a reckless driver and weather conditions were poor. But I knew that she wouldn't even have been on that road, at that time, if it hadn't been for the note Carrie and I stuck under the napkin holder on the counter at the Minuette.

Meet me at the old skating pond at four o'clock.

(signed) *Your secret admirer*

CHAPTER THIRTEEN

The movie Greg took me to see after dinner was a good movie; even so I found my mind wandering. I didn't want to think anymore about Max or about Bonnie's accident. But I couldn't get either one out of my mind. Greg made a few comments about the movie as we drove home. He asked me if I would like to stop somewhere for a snack, but it was late and I really didn't feel like eating anything.

"Can we do this again sometime, ma'am?" He put on a funny western drawl as we said goodnight.

"Sure thing, pardner."

That made him laugh, although I didn't feel as lighthearted and witty as I sounded. I felt tired and confused and cheated. I shouldn't have had to think about anything except having a good time with Greg. He was about the nicest boy I'd ever known. Yet over our evening there hung an unpleasant sense of things I didn't understand, a foreboding of . . . of what?

It was nearly midnight. Carrie and Aunt Lorna were in bed, but Mom was reading in the living room. Waiting up for me. After all, we were in a strange town and I was out with a boy she didn't really know. It was comforting to see her there in the lamplight, lifting her head and smiling across the living room toward where I stood in the doorway.

"How was the movie?"

"Oh — good, real good."

She closed her book. It was late and we were both tired. I looked at her across the space that separated us, thinking how she was always there when I needed her . . . and how now I couldn't tell her what was on my mind.

"Greg seems like a nice young man," she said.

"He is." I nodded automatically. "He's real nice."

She smiled, and I wondered what she would think if she knew what Carrie and I had done. What would she think of me? What we had done wasn't so terrible in itself — but it sure had terrible results. What would Mom think of me if she knew?

I wanted to tell her. I was exhausted with the burden of the secret. She didn't know I was having this struggle with myself, and as I took a step toward her, almost ready to tell the secret — promise to Carrie or not — she was looking away, rising from the chair and lifting her hand to turn off the lamp.

"I'll go up with you," she said. "I think it's past my bedtime."

The wrist I had hurt was my left wrist, so I could still write. But the words came slowly.

Dear Diary — Had a date tonight with Greg Preston. He remembers me from way last winter when he saw me in the Minuette with Carrie.

I was going to write about our date, dinner at the Blue Moon Inn and the movie, but I sat staring at the words I had written about the Minuette, and writing about dinner and the movie didn't seem important. Max watching Carrie and me as we left the Minuette kept coming back to my mind.

Why did he ask Janette about us? Had he overheard Carrie and me talking, overheard us composing the note for Bonnie?

The thought startled me. Had we been so silly and carried away with our idea that we forgot to whisper? How could we have been so dumb! Vainly I tried to remember if we had kept our voices low . . . if anyone had been in the booths around us . . . or at a nearby table.

But it had been six months, and my memory of that afternoon was vague. Mostly what I remembered, and that I remembered clearly enough, was our own booth: the two cups of tea, Carrie's spiral notebook, the feel of the pencil in my fingers, Carrie watching as I composed the note. "You sign it." I pushed the slip of paper across the formica top toward Carrie. Her hair hung across her cheeks as she bent her head over the note.

Did Max overhear us? And if he did overhear, would he care what silly thing we were up to?

Maybe he would care, if he knew Bonnie Vayle.

I tried to remember more about the afternoon at the Minuette. I tried to remember seeing Max there, but I couldn't; I couldn't remember seeing any particular person. Even the two men with the checkerboard were just two men in a booth; I hadn't even looked at their faces. Beyond the booth where Carrie and I were writing our note to Bonnie, the rest of the room around us was only an indistinct background of occasional voices, the clink of silverware and dishes.

Well, there had been Janette. I did remember her. She brought our tea . . . but that was before we got our idea about writing the note. I had a vague memory of Janette passing our booth now and then to wait on customers.

According to Greg, Bonnie and Janette had

been best friends. Janette would probably know if Bonnie and Max knew each other.

I sat and thought about that. I wanted to talk to Carrie, but it was too late to wake her up. Morning would be time enough.

I felt tired, and yet keyed-up at the same time. Thoughts began to crowd into my mind. Even if I couldn't talk to Carrie till morning I was pretty sure she'd agree with me: All the things that had happened around the house — the chair, the door slamming closed, the feeling she had of being followed and watched — had happened since Joseph died, as she said. They had also happened since Max came to be the gardener and handyman.

The night was warm, but I shivered as I recalled how he watched Carrie and me as we came walking from the woods. Did he guess we were coming from the ravine?

Nothing had happened to anybody in the house except to Carrie, until I came. Aunt Lorna had no problems. Pearl was happy. Then I came and I felt the same way Carrie did, uneasy, watched . . . pursued down the stairs by a chair. Nothing had really happened to anyone except Carrie and me. And Joseph. Joseph died. And because Joseph died, Max got his job.

I closed my diary. There was nothing more I wanted to write tonight. My thoughts had already traveled a million miles from dinner at the Blue Moon Inn and the movie afterward.

But even after I got into bed, I couldn't stop thinking, trying to figure things out. Did Max know Bonnie? If he heard us composing our note, luring Bonnie out on Green Oak Road on a stormy afternoon, maybe he would blame us for her death and want to hurt us to get revenge.

I drew the bed covers closer up around myself, feeling lost and afraid. Max had been only a few feet from my window when Carrie called to me about the phone. He could easily have heard her call. Had he been bold enough to come into the house while I was on the phone, sneak up the back stairway, and then push me when I started downstairs? Push me and then throw the chair after me as I stumbled to my feet?

It was almost too fantastic to imagine. It was a crazy thing for him to do. He could have been discovered any moment. "Why, Max?" I could hear Aunt Lorna's surprised voice. "What are you doing here in the house?"

Maybe not so crazy. Maybe sometimes he did work inside the house. He was handyman as well as gardener.

But it *was* crazy, I insisted to myself. On that particular afternoon he was cleaning out gutters. He had no reason to be in the house.

I lay staring at the night shadows on the ceiling of my room. My wrist still hurt, and the hard jolt of falling down the stairs was still in my mind.

I was too keyed-up to sleep. I wanted morning to come. I would tell Carrie about Max watching us as we left the Minuette. I'd tell her I thought we had more to worry about from Max than from Joseph's ghost.

Then Carrie and I would go to the Minuette and ask Janette if her friend Bonnie had known a young man named Max.

I planned it all carefully.

It was three o'clock when I looked at the bedside clock. In a couple of hours it would start to get light outside. I'd just stay awake and soon it would be morning and I could talk to Carrie.

But I fell asleep at last, Aunt Lorna's words echoing in my memory . . . *highly recommended . . . has a green thumb.*

In my sleep I saw Max coming toward me, ominous, staring, holding up his hands for me to see, fingers spread, thumbs green.

CHAPTER
FOURTEEN

I had fallen asleep late, and I woke late. It was after eleven. I looked sleepily at the clock, and blurry memories came into focus gradually as I sat up in bed. My date with Greg and our conversation about Max, then my own thoughts after I had come home.

My deductions and decision of the night before rushed back over me. Everything I had thought about the night before hung like a painting in my mind.

I wanted to see Carrie, talk to her, tell her what I thought; that was the first thing.

And after that?

I pulled on jeans and the first top I came to in the closet. When I looked at myself in the mirror before I went downstairs, I thought I looked unnaturally excited and anxious.

Maybe no one would notice.

* * *

Aunt Lorna was in the hallway as I came down, watering the large philodendron by the front door. She looked fresh and cool in a pale green cotton dress. Mom was on the porch. Carrie was gone.

"She drove off about half an hour ago," Mom answered absently. She was working a crossword; I could see the newspaper folded neatly to the puzzle page.

"Drove off? Where?"

Of all times for Carrie to go away, just when I needed to talk to her!

Mom shook her head. "She didn't say."

I drank a glass of orange juice and sat on the porch steps thinking what to do now. By and by Carrie would be back, I only had to be patient and wait. But I didn't feel patient.

As I watched, Max drove into the driveway and parked back near the garage. Aunt Lorna must have been watching for him, because she came out right away and went over to the car. Max was taking small bushes from the trunk of his car, spikey little twigs with burlap wrapped around the roots.

I had an impulse to get away from the house — and now was the best time, with Max and Aunt Lorna busy with the rosebushes, and Mom lost in her crossword.

"I'm just going to take a little walk," I murmured, and Mom barely glanced up. "That's nice," she said. She loved her crosswords, and I probably could have said I was flying to the moon.

I thought about going back into the house to get my purse and sunglasses, but by the time I did that and came back downstairs, it would be just my luck that Aunt Lorna would be coming in from the garden. "Where are you off to?" she'd ask cheerfully. I just wanted to go without any fuss. If I started toward Rowen Avenue, maybe I'd meet Carrie coming home and I'd tell her my plan and then we could drive to the Minuette together. We could ask Janette if Bonnie and Max were friends. After that, well, after that I wasn't sure what Carrie and I should do. I could figure that out as I walked along.

I went down the porch steps and along the driveway toward the street. As I neared the end of the driveway I wanted to turn around and look back. I wanted to see if Max was watching me. I could feel someone watching me. They say you can tell if someone is staring at you. I forced myself not to turn around. I just kept walking, turning at the end of the driveway and starting toward the main part of town. Green Oak Lane lay ahead, basking in the summer sunlight, houses set back from the street, shaded, half hidden by trees.

Was Max still watching? I knew someone was. Someone was watching me. If you look at someone long enough, they'll turn around. Ginny and I used to try that in school, for fun, and it usually worked. We'd pick a boy in class we thought was cute, and stare at the back of his head. Usually, sooner or later, he'd turn around with sort of an uncertain look, like something was wrong. The trick was to glance away at the last second, so he couldn't really tell it was you looking at him.

Was that why Max was staring after me, to make me nervous and jumpy and finally make me turn around to look back at him?

Well, I wasn't going to look back. I kept right on walking, looking straight ahead, and in a few more steps I knew I was hidden from sight by a row of tall lilac bushes growing close to the sidewalk. After that there was no way anyone from Aunt Lorna's house could see me. I drew a breath of relief, and looked hopefully on up ahead to see if I could see Carrie driving along toward home.

There was a delivery truck pulling out of a driveway, and a couple of grade school boys on bicycles; but otherwise Green Oak Lane was deserted. There weren't even any parked cars on the street, as everybody used their driveways. Leafy elms arched over the sidewalks, and I was grateful for the shade. It was a warm day, and growing warmer.

I knew it was a long walk from Aunt Lorna's to the Minuette. I remembered that only too well. If I didn't meet Carrie, I'd have to walk all the way, and maybe back again. At any rate, it wouldn't be as bad as walking on a cold winter night.

I tried to get my thoughts in order and make up my mind just what I'd say to Janette. I was so intent on this, and watching ahead for Carrie, I didn't notice that a car was coming along the street behind me. Just as I caught the sound of tires and realized there was a car very close, I heard a voice.

"Want a ride?"

I saw the dark blue car at the curb just as the words were spoken.

It was Max.

The street was suddenly no longer sunny and peaceful and pretty. It was silent and deserted, with not a soul in sight anywhere. The delivery truck was long gone. The boys on their bicycles were gone too. There was no one anywhere on the long stretch of Green Oak Lane but Max and me.

"Come on, I'm going your way."

I kept walking as I glanced over at the car and shook my head. I couldn't see the expression of Max's eyes because of his dark glasses — and I wished I had my glasses so he couldn't see my face or read my expression. I felt exposed without my sunglasses.

"I like to walk, thanks." I hoped I sounded nonchalant. My voice sounded strained to me.

"Going to town?"

I knew "to town" meant the business section. I didn't answer.

"It's a long walk. Come on, have a ride."

"No thanks." I shook my head again. The car crawled along at a snail's pace to stay even with me.

"It's a hot day for such a long walk."

When I didn't answer, he didn't say anything for a moment. But he was still inching along to stay even with me.

"Your aunt sent me — she said you shouldn't walk all the way to town by yourself."

Was that true? My thoughts faltered. Was it Aunt Lorna who had been watching me leave, and then told Max to give me a ride? No; it was a lie, I was sure. He would have mentioned Aunt Lorna right away.

I felt frightened as the car crept along at the curb. Max was silent now. In a way, that was worse than his urging me to get into the car.

I wanted to say something casual to show him I wasn't frightened — "I need the exercise," or "tell Aunt Lorna thanks anyway," something like that. But I couldn't get any words out. My mouth was clamped shut. Maybe if I opened it, I would scream — and there was nobody to hear me on peaceful, quiet Green Oak Lane. Aunt Lorna loved her little village because it was peaceful and quiet. Well, it was *too* peaceful and quiet for me! I wanted crowds of people milling about, and lots of cars tooting their horns, and drivers shouting at Max to speed it up and stop causing a traffic jam.

Where is everybody, I thought desperately. *Please, somebody come out of a house.*

Nobody came out of a house, but as though in answer to my prayers a couple of joggers appeared from a side street and turned onto Green Oak Lane about half a block ahead of me. They were plump ladies, not jogging very fast. As I kept walking they were running slower and slower, and about the time I was close enough to hear, one of them said, "That's all I can do today." Then they both slowed down to a walk. I stayed a few yards behind them, and after the ladies turned around and looked at Max in his car and whispered together, he stepped on the accelerator and drove on down the street.

The women turned and peeked back at me curiously, and I tried to look like I hadn't noticed any car following me.

At the next corner the women parted, going toward houses on opposite sides of the street. "See you tomorrow," one of them called, and the other turned and waved before she went into her house.

But I was not alone again. By now I was almost to Rowen Avenue. The houses were not separated by such wide yards and woody stretches. There was some traffic turning off

Rowen Avenue, and there were children playing in a playground at one corner.

There was no sign of Carrie, which was too bad. I really wanted her with me when I went into the Minuette.

But there was no sign of Max either, and I was grateful for that.

I turned on Rowen Avenue, at the corner where Mom and I had turned when we first came to town. It was only a few days ago, but it seemed like a long time.

I could soon see the Minuette in the block ahead, its green awning stretched above the front windows.

I began to walk more slowly. I had been so concerned about Max I hadn't thought much about what I was really going to do and say now that I was here.

I hadn't seen Janette since Christmas. She wouldn't remember me. I'd be some weird girl asking questions about Bonnie, and maybe Janette wouldn't want to talk about Bonnie.

And what if Janette wasn't even working today? I hadn't thought of that until this moment. Everybody has days off. Nobody works every day. I didn't think I could bear to wait, if she wasn't there. But I wouldn't have any choice but to wait.

I tried to look in the Minuette window as I walked toward the door, but reflections on the glass made it hard to see inside. I could see myself looking in better than I could see anything else.

I opened the door, and at first I didn't see Janette. Then I saw her coming from the kitchen with a tray of plates. The noontime rush was over, but the coffee shop was about half filled. None of the customers really paid any attention as I came in, but I felt like everyone was looking, looking at this girl all by herself.

CHAPTER
FIFTEEN

I sat down at the end of the counter furthest from the other customers so I could talk to Janette as privately as possible. There was another waitress working too, and I hoped she wouldn't be the one to wait on me. I was glad to see Janette coming toward my end of the counter.

"Hi, there." Her voice was cheery, but I was sure she didn't recognize me. After all, it had been six months. And she didn't have any special reason to remember me.

Nevertheless she looked at me thoughtfully as she set out a glass of water and silverware.

"Don't I know you?"

Her face was exactly as I remembered it, dimpled, dark-eyed. *Someday*, I thought, *she'll be doing something more interesting than waiting on customers in a small town diner.*

"Maybe you do remember me." I took the menu she offered and held it without opening it. "It's been a while. I was in here a couple

130

of times last Christmas with my cousin Carrie."

Janette tilted her head, and I could see she was trying to think back to last Christmastime.

"Tom Abbott was with us one time."

I waited to see if this helped.

"Maybe you don't know him?"

Janette smiled. "Sure I know Tom. He's a nice guy."

"He goes with my cousin Carrie."

"Carrie Thatcher. Sure, I know her — and you're her cousin?"

"Right."

After that Janette stood nodding and smiling at me, waiting for me to say something more if I wanted to. I rubbed my fingers on the corners of the plastic-coated menu I was holding. What should I order . . . what should I say. . . ?

"I was talking to Greg Preston last night."

"Oh, yeah, I know Greg," Janette said. "He comes in here a lot."

I seized that. "He likes it here. He told me."

Janette looked pleased.

"He — he also told me you were good friends with Bonnie Vayle."

It was abrupt-sounding, and I knew it. I was stirring up sad memories. I was sorry to do that. But I needed to. I just wished Carrie was with me, and I wanted Janette not to be hurt or feel bad because I mentioned Bonnie.

"She was my best friend." There was a forlorn note in Janette's voice. Her dark eyes grew serious. "She died in a car accident."

Tell me about it!

A man and woman came in and sat in a booth near our end of the counter.

"I'll be right back," Janette said companionably. She sounded like she was willing to come back and talk to me about Bonnie. I watched as she went to the booth and gave glasses of water to the customers.

She wrote their order on the order pad she kept in her apron pocket.

Why was I alone here in a coffee shop hundreds of miles from home asking questions about a dead girl I had never really even known?

Beyond the Minuette window I watched the traffic on Rowen Avenue. It wasn't hard and heavy traffic, but it was continuous. There was always some car or van or delivery truck to see.

When Janette came back to my place at the counter, I'd had some time to think.

"Know what you want?" she asked.

She was thinking about the menu, but I wasn't.

"Your girl friend Bonnie, she had a lot of boyfriends, didn't she?" I looked at Janette as innocently as I could.

"Boyfriends! She sure did. She was about the most popular girl in school."

That sounded logical. I remembered how pretty Bonnie was and how easily she got along with boys.

And now it was time for the big question.

"Did she ever have a boyfriend named Max?"

"Max?" Janette made a face. "Not him, not Max."

"But she knew him?"

"Oh, sure she knew him. And he liked her a lot. He was a little older, out of school. She met him at Louie's one night."

"Louie's?" This was a place I hadn't heard of.

"You know Louie's. It's just down the street a few blocks."

No, I thought, *I don't know Louie's. I don't live here in Rowenville, remember?*

"Bonnie was at Louie's on a date," Janette continued, "and this guy Max flirted with her and maybe she flirted back a little, but she didn't really like him. Actually he got to be kind of a pest, calling her up all the time, things like that."

I listened to Janette with fascination. *What is Louie's?* I wondered. *A pizza place, bowling alley, bar?* Max had flirted with Bonnie, and maybe she had flirted back, though she didn't particularly like him. It was a lot to think about.

And then Janette said something that surprised me completely.

"The fella Bonnie was crazy about was Dan."

Dan? Who was he? Carrie and I had thought Bonnie was trying to steal Tom away from Carrie — and all the time she was crazy about someone named Dan?

"Who's Dan?" I looked at Janette blankly.

"He's the manager out at the Blue Moon Inn, and he's gorgeous." Janette lifted her eyebrows. "He was crazy about Bonnie too."

So that was his name. Dan. The handsome young man who had come to our table that day after Christmas when Aunt Lorna took us to eat at the Blue Moon Inn. "Did you enjoy your meal?" he had asked, while Carrie and I locked eyes across the table and sent the silent isn't-he-handsome messages to each other. When he walked on to other tables, Aunt Lorna had said he was the new manager. Apparently he was still at the Blue Moon even though I hadn't seen him when I was with Greg.

I didn't know exactly what to say next. I felt Janette wanted to help me, but she didn't know what I was after. She couldn't know the answer to the question that was on my mind more fervently than ever: Did Max know we wrote that note to Bonnie?

I ordered a Coke and sank against the back of the stool. When I finished the Coke I'd have to walk back along Green Oak Lane. What if Max showed up again? I felt worn out trying to figure everything out. And I wasn't eager to start home.

I made the Coke last as long as I could. When I was ready to leave, the Minuette had emptied out some and Janette was sitting at the cash register.

And then I realized I didn't have any money with me. My purse was still back at Aunt Lorna's house. How could I have forgotten that! I felt so stupid and embarrassed I didn't know what to do, but Janette just laughed and said not to worry about it.

"Carrie's in here with Tom a lot — she'll pay me."

I thought that was very nice of Janette. Once again I was sure every eye in the room was on me, the girl with the red face!

I went out to Rowen Avenue, grateful to escape the scene of this embarrassment. The afternoon had grown even warmer. And overcast. The air was humid. At once my fears about Max were realized as I saw his car coming toward me. Even though I'd been wondering if I would see him, I was startled. Before I could run away the car was at the curb in front of the Minuette.

Even more startling was Carrie's face at the passenger window.

"Get in, Elizabeth," she said. "Please get in."

CHAPTER SIXTEEN

The desperation in Carrie's voice frightened me. I stared at her and she said again, "Please get in, Elizabeth." Her expression was fearful, imploring. "He has a gun."

"Get in the back." Max's voice was low and rough. He was close beside Carrie in the front seat of the car. As he leaned toward me I could see light glinting on the dark glasses he wore.

I grasped the back handle and yanked the door open. As I got in, Max barely gave me time to close the door before the car sped off along Rowen Avenue.

Carrie twisted around to look at me over her shoulder, and I leaned toward her. "Carrie — where have you been? Where did you go?"

"You were sleeping late, so I thought I'd shop a little — I came out of a store, and there was Max."

Her voice trembled as she spoke, and she glanced toward Max.

"Shut up."

Max's right arm moved, and I knew he was jabbing Carrie with the gun he held. He drove with his left hand only, and as I looked out, dazed and scared, I saw that we were on Green Oak Lane. Was he taking us home? I couldn't believe I was in a car with someone who had a gun, a real gun . . . and was driving us home?

But Aunt Lorna's house went by in a flash. Max didn't even look at it. Carrie shrank down in the front seat and put her hands over her face.

And then we were out of town, speeding through the countryside between columns of trees that formed the woods. On either side of the road trees stretched ahead as far as I could see.

I watched helplessly as the woods and roadway flashed by. My mind felt like it was spinning in a thousand directions, and at the same time like it was empty of a single thought. I could see the back of Max's head, and I knew he wasn't worried about me: One wrong move from me and he would shoot the gun he had jammed against Carrie's side. He was still driving with only his left hand on the steering wheel. In the rearview mirror I could see the edge of his forehead and the dark sunglasses. If he was looking back at me, I couldn't tell.

Suddenly, as we rounded a curve, I saw the Blue Moon Inn a short distance ahead. It was an off-time for business, but there were a few cars in the parking lot. Everyone inside was safe, happy, enjoying good food . . . we flashed by even faster than we'd gone by Aunt Lorna's house.

Help, I wanted to cry to the empty cars in the parking lot, to the silent facade of the Blue Moon Inn.

But we were past in a moment. The Blue Moon Inn was behind us. The woods filled up the sides of the roadway again, now darkening the road with shadows as the road narrowed and the woods grew more dense.

Then I felt the car slowing. Max pulled off to the side of the road and drove the car a short way across a grassy spot that ended by a pond. It was the skating pond Aunt Lorna had shown us at Christmastime. It was also the place where Carrie and I had asked Bonnie to come in our note:

Meet me at the old skating pond at four o'clock.

Carrie felt the car stopping and took her hands away from her face. We both looked at the shore of the pond where the car had stopped. The pond was shallow, dull blue in the shaded light of the woods. The surface of the water was calm, undisturbed by any breeze, reflecting the heavy branches of over-hanging trees.

On the far side of the pond, the old warming house was overgrown with weeds and creeping vines. Jagged edges of broken glass hung at the window frames. The light in the woods was dim, greenish, mysterious. So different from the cold, icy, winter-white day we had been at the skating pond with Aunt Lorna. But it was the same place.

"Why did you bring us here?" Carrie's voice was trembling with fear and confusion.

I thought I knew, somehow, why we were here. But Carrie didn't know about Max and Bonnie. She only wanted to know why we had been brought to a pond in the woods.

"Get out."

Max nudged the gun at Carrie, and she pushed open the car door and stumbled out into the grass and weeds at the edge of the pond. Tears glistened in her eyes. Her day had begun so pleasantly: Cousin Elizabeth was sleeping late after a lovely date, so Carrie would go into town to shop.

Get in the car. Max was suddenly there when she came out of a store.

I knew all that. I knew it as clearly as if I had been there.

And then, suddenly, there was the gun. Carrie wouldn't expect that on a quiet, summer afternoon on Rowen Avenue.

Now as she got out of the car and stood by the pond, Max twisted in the front seat and pointed the gun toward me.

"You too. Out."

I opened the car door and got out on the bank of the pond beside Carrie. She clung to my arm, and we stood there cold with fear on a hot summer day, watching as Max opened the door on his side of the car and came around toward us, holding the gun.

"I know what you two were up to," he was saying as he walked toward us. "I heard you talking about Bonnie, I heard you writing that note."

His expression was hidden by the dark glasses, but I looked at him as though I was hypnotized. He *had* overheard us in the Minuette. He *had* overheard us writing the note to Bonnie. He knew it was our fault Bonnie was on Green Oak Road that snowy afternoon. He knew it was our fault she died.

Max came toward us, menacingly in the leafy shadows of the woods. I wanted to run, but my legs were too weak to move, the way they are sometimes in a dream. Carrie's hand clutched my arm, fingernails digging into my skin.

"I heard you," Max said, stepping closer to us. "You wrote her that note. She's dead because of you. It's your fault."

"It's *not* our fault," Carrie cried out. "It's *not* our fault." She grasped my arm more tightly, trying to draw me back away from Max as he came toward us with the gun.

I tried to think of something to *do*, something to outwit Max, escape somehow, or get his gun away from him, *something*. But everything I thought of was useless: grabbing the gun, screaming for help, running off to hide in the woods. None of that would work. I looked back into those dark glasses that told me nothing, and my heart sank.

And then we heard a car approaching on the road, approaching and turning off, just as Max had done; turning off Green Oak Road and coming toward the pond.

Max turned his head, looking away from us for a moment as he listened to the approaching car.

CHAPTER
SEVENTEEN

The car that jolted to a stop beside the pond was the same car that had whisked me off to dinner at the Blue Moon Inn the night before. Greg Preston got out on the driver's side and stood there, looking at us across the hood of his car.

"What's going on?"

Max maneuvered around so that he could keep all three of us in gun-range. I didn't know what Greg could do to help us, with a gun pointed at him, but he was *there*. Carrie and I weren't alone anymore. It was something.

"I said, what's going on?" Greg's tone was amazingly firm for someone facing a gun, but I could see that his face was pale under his tan.

Max didn't answer right away. He stood looking at Greg, sizing up the situation. Finally he said, "I just gave these girls a ride. They said they wanted a ride. Isn't that right?" The gun moved toward us.

"They wouldn't do that." Greg stared straight back at Max. "I know Elizabeth wouldn't ask you for a ride, and I don't think Carrie would either."

Max didn't answer. Carrie and I stood like statues. Around us the woods were silent.

Then Greg said, "Janette told me she saw Elizabeth get into your car, and I knew Elizabeth wouldn't do that on her own."

Greg remembered how I thought Max was creepy! He remembered! Oh, thank you for remembering, Greg!

But what would happen now?

Greg didn't try to come around the car toward us. I knew he was as tense and uncertain of what to do as Carrie and I were.

"I was lucky," Greg said. "I picked up your car on Green Oak Lane. What I haven't figured out is why you came here." He glanced at the trees and the weather-beaten old warming house.

"Because this is where their note said." There was a tone of cunning in Max's voice.

"Their note?" I knew Greg didn't have any idea what note Max was talking about. He was stalling for time.

"Their note to Bonnie. Meet me at the old skating pond." Max repeated the words of the note ominously. "That's where she was going when she died. It was all their fault."

143

From somewhere deep in the woods a bird called, and then everything was quiet again.

"Bonnie was my girl, she liked me a lot," Max said proudly. "She wanted me to get even for her, get even with these two. So now I'm getting even."

"Wait —" Greg started to protest, and Max lifted his gun and fired into the sky above the pond.

No one moved. Not Greg, not Carrie, not me.

The shot reverberated in the air and I thought everyone in the world had heard it. But nobody came racing up the road to rescue us. The sound of the gunshot faded, and it was once again Max and Greg and Carrie and me alone in the silent woods.

"I thought about it," Max said slyly. "I'm smart. I don't rush into things. I think them out. People rush into things and they get them all wrong. Not me. I thought about it and I worked out a plan."

Below the dark glasses his mouth formed a sneering kind of smile.

"You know what my plan was? Be the gardener, that was my plan."

He paused again and laughed a funny, high-pitched laugh.

"Get rid of that old man and be the gardener."

He's crazy, I thought. He's really crazy. Crazy enough to kill us all.

"Cat and mouse!" Max shouted suddenly. "That's what we've been playing, isn't that right?"

He was ignoring Greg, speaking to Carrie and me now.

"You like my little game of cat and mouse?" He jiggled the gun to stir up our memories. Whatever he had done, he wanted us to know he had done it. I darted a quick glance at Carrie. Her eyes were wide with terror.

"You?"

Carrie's voice was so low I think Max only guessed at what she said. But he answered her.

"Yeah. Me."

There was an arrogance in his voice. At will he had gone in and out of Aunt Lorna's house, boldly, undetected. All the things that Carrie had told me about, the feeling of being watched, followed; that was Max. The voice calling her name as the door of her room slammed shut, the chair thrown down the stairs toward her as she stood in the hallway reading her mother's note, the news clipping of Joseph in her book. It was all Max.

Carrie didn't even know about the torn snapshot I had found in the doll's lap. I knew Max had done that too.

In memory I saw his head lift as he was working on the gutters and Carrie called, "Phone for you, Elizabeth." I felt the push of the chair against my back. I saw the chair coming down toward me, swift and deadly. And it was all Max.

Carrie and I drew closer together, and Greg took a step forward beside his car.

"Stay back." Max turned the gun on Greg.

Greg lifted his hands and held them out like someone about to explain something. "Hey, listen, Max. You don't know the whole story."

Max didn't answer.

Greg moved toward the door of his car. He kept a wary eye on Max and the gun. "Wait a minute, see what I've got to show you."

He reached in through the open car window and took a small notebook from the front seat. He held the notebook toward Max.

"What's that?" Max didn't move.

"Something I think you'd like to read." Greg gestured with the notebook again, but Max didn't move.

"You read it to me."

Greg waited a moment and then slowly opened the notebook. He ruffled the pages, looking for the one he wanted.

Then he began to read.

"Max called again tonight. I wish he'd stop that. He's a pest."

* * *

Greg looked up at Max.

"Bonnie's diary," he explained.

I could sense Max tighten up when Greg said that. He didn't say anything. The gun was still pointed straight at Greg. I was fascinated and bewildered. How had Greg gotten hold of Bonnie Vayle's diary! My mind was spinning again.

"There's more." Greg turned a few pages in the notebook. "Here's an entry for December 27th, the day before she died."

He looked across at Max, to see if he wanted to hear it.

"Read it."

Greg glanced at me. I'm sure I looked small and frightened. His expression seemed to say, "Hang on, don't be afraid."

"December 27th," Greg read from the diary. "I have a date with Dan tomorrow afternoon. He's off at four and I'm meeting him at the Blue Moon."

Greg looked up from the diary.

"Bonnie didn't care about you, Max. Not enough for you to make all this trouble for yourself. She wasn't coming out here to the skating pond that afternoon, she was just on her way to the Blue Moon Inn to meet Dan."

"But they wrote the note." Max swerved the gun toward Carrie and me. "They told her to come here."

He took a few steps backward, still keeping us all in gun range.

"They wrote the note — they told her to come here —"

Greg stepped toward us, still holding the notebook.

"Bonnie thought *you* wrote that note, Max. Janette gave it to her at the Minuette, and Bonnie said, 'A secret admirer! I bet that's Max,' and then she tore up the note and tossed it into the trash bin behind the counter."

Max stared at Greg, trying to make sense out of what Greg had said.

And I was trying to make sense of it too.

Bonnie thought *Max* had written the note? Bonnie tore up the note. . .?

"Stay away from me," Max cried out suddenly, although no one had moved toward him. "Stay away from me."

He moved abruptly past Carrie and me and threw open the door of his car. We watched in stunned silence as he lunged into the car, gunned the engine, and backed recklessly out of the clearing toward the road.

CHAPTER EIGHTEEN

We didn't dare move for a few moments, hardly dared believe that Max was really truly gone and we were alone and safe.

The sound of his car faded into the distance and then there was nothing more to be heard.

"Come on!" Greg was the first to move into action. "We'll get back to a phone and notify the police."

I found that my legs would move after all, and Carrie and I scrambled into Greg's car, wide-eyed with excitement at our close brush with terror. When Greg had turned the car and driven back onto the road, he reached over and took my hand.

"You okay?"

I nodded, and he looked back toward Carrie.

"You okay back there?"

Carrie's voice sounded trembly, but she said she was okay.

There was no sign of Max's car in either direction, but we knew from the sound of his car when he left that he had headed away from town. "We'll get to a phone and notify the police," Greg said, as he turned toward town and we sped along the deserted road.

"Where did you get Bonnie's diary?" There were a lot of questions I wanted to ask, but that was number one.

Greg loosened my hand long enough to pick up the notebook which he had tossed on the seat between us. He handed it to me without a word, but I didn't open it right away. I didn't feel right opening someone else's diary.

"Go ahead," Greg said. "Open it."

I turned the pages with amazement. It was a record of gasoline purchases, oil changes, and car mileage.

"But —" I looked at Greg, shaking my head. "But —"

"How did I know about Bonnie tearing up the note, and going to meet Dan at the inn?" He knew the questions in my mind. "Janette told me. After Bonnie died. Janette told me Bonnie tore up a note she thought Max had written. And she told me Bonnie was on her way to the Blue Moon Inn to meet Dan the day she had the accident."

I turned to look back at Carrie. Bonnie had

been on her way to the Blue Moon Inn. She wasn't on her way to meet a 'secret admirer' at the skating pond. She'd thrown our note away. The burden of guilt over the accident was gone. After all those months, our regret and guilt were suddenly gone. It wasn't our fault. *It wasn't our fault.*

The Blue Moon Inn appeared ahead, and Greg pulled into the parking lot. But he didn't bother parking. He drove right up to the front door and jammed on the brakes.

"We'll phone the police from here."

He was already out of the car, and Carrie and I hurried after him, across the cobblestones and through the dark oak merrie-olde-England door. It was dim inside, air-conditioned and delightfully cool. Through the archway at the end of the foyer we could see a few people lingering at tables for a late lunch, but there was a subdued atmosphere compared to the noise and bustle there had been the night before when I had dinner with Greg.

There was a public phone at one side of the foyer, and Greg had the police department in a matter of moments. The hostess, who had come to meet us with a pleasant smile, stood listening curiously to what she could hear of Greg's phone call. Carrie and I sank down on chairs in the foyer and Carrie whispered, "I still feel all shaky." I nodded to show I felt shaky too, and then Greg hung up the phone and came to where we were sitting.

"The police are coming right out," he said. "Might as well wait in here where it's so cool."

The hostess had faded away, but reappeared almost at once with the handsome young manager. Carrie and I stared with special interest now. We knew his name was Dan and he had been dating Bonnie Vayle. He couldn't know what an important part he had played in our lives.

"Is there anything I can do to help?" he wanted to know, and then he stood talking to Greg and the hostess asked Carrie and me if we would like something cool to drink. I'm sure we looked hot and flustered and scared to death. But we were still too excited to settle down and drink iced tea or Cokes, so we just shook our heads and said, "No, thank you."

It wasn't long before a police car came racing out from town. Greg saw it first, as he stood with Dan at the window beside the front door. We all trooped outside, and the car pulled into the Blue Moon Inn driveway.

The two policemen were quick to get essential details from us, and then asked us to go to the Rowenville station to file the charges against Max. They said they had alerted the police in neighboring towns, and were going on themselves toward Arbor Heights, the next town that lay on the route Max had taken.

The siren was screaming as the police car sped off, and we all stood watching until it was out of sight and the sound of the siren was lost in the distance.

We wouldn't learn until evening that Max was finally caught, eighty miles away in the town of Ridgemont. And it was a lot longer than that before the charges against him for Joseph's murder and for kidnapping Carrie and me were heard in court and Max was sent to the state mental hospital for psychiatric treatment.

All that was in the future, as we stood on the steps of the Blue Moon Inn and listened to the police siren going off through the woods on Green Oak Road.

"Let's go tell your mothers what happened," Greg said, "and then we can go on to the police station and see what has to be done there."

Dan and the hostess and several curious customers had clustered in the doorway, and they watched us drive away. As I settled back, I saw Greg's car-upkeep record book still lying on the car seat where I had put it.

"Where did you get the idea to read this to Max like it was Bonnie's diary?" I asked, lifting up the book.

Greg still looked tense, but he managed a grin. "Doesn't everyone keep some kind of diary?"

"I do," Carrie's voice came from the back seat.

Greg was looking at me, waiting for me to answer.

I thought about my diary, tucked in the drawer of the writing table in my room at Aunt Lorna's house.

"Yes, I guess everyone does."

Greg was holding my hand again, and it felt good. I thought he was the most wonderful boy I had ever known. And I wanted to go on knowing him. There were several more weeks remaining of my Rowenville visit, and after that? Somehow I was sure "after that" would include Greg.

Aunt Lorna's was in sight. The skies had cleared and the house was nestled in the dappled sunshine. The apple orchard was filled with golden light. As I saw it there on Green Oak Lane, I felt the charm and beauty of the house that I had first felt and then lost.

I knew it would be a while before I could completely separate the house from unhappy memories of the Christmas visit and Bonnie's death, but Greg's hand holding mine was the beginning of new and happier times. I was glad to be there, again.